MALARIA

Susan Hillmore is a painter and novelist, living in Gloucestershire. She studied Fine Art at Camberwell School of Art. Her first novel, *The Greenhouse*, was shortlisted for the *Sunday Express* Book of the Year.

Susan Hillmore

MALARIA

VINTAGE

Published by Vintage 2001

2 4 6 8 10 9 7 5 3 1

First published in Great Britain in 2000 by
Jonathan Cape

Vintage
Random House, 20 Vauxhall Bridge Road,
London SW1V 2SA

Random House Australia (Pty) Limited
20 Alfred Street, Milsons Point, Sydney
New South Wales 2061, Australia

Random House New Zealand Limited
18 Poland Road, Glenfield, Auckland 10,
New Zealand

Random House (Pty) Limited
Endulini, 5A Jubilee Road, Parktown 2193,
South Africa

The Random House Group Limited Reg. No. 954009
www.randomhouse.co.uk

A CIP catalogue record for this book
is available from the British Library

ISBN 0 09 928334 4

Papers used by Random House are natural, recyclable
products made from wood grown in sustainable forests.
The manufacturing processes conform to the environmental regulations of the country of origin

Printed and bound in Great Britain by
Bookmarque Ltd, Croydon, Surrey

To

D.M.B.   S.P.B.

& R.H.

One

Mannar was an enchanted place. Of all inhabited islands in the world it was for centuries considered to be a Garden of Eden. Turtles played on its tropical shores and snow leopard stalked the foothills of its only mountain. Sparkling streams cascaded down hillsides and meandered through green valleys, where ebony and mahogany grew into dark forests. Rivers wove between mangroves into fertile estuaries filled with crustaceans and poured out into the ocean. Shoals of coloured fish fed on coral banks. Trees dripped odorous gums and balms. Leaves of the ironwood tree coloured silks and cottons. Fruits staved off famine. Elephants browsed with deer and roamed in peace. Cranes and pink-headed duck reflected their plumage in water tanks built by kings on the fringes of ancient cities. Monkeys chattered as they sated themselves on nuts from plantations. Bee-eaters inhabited jungle clearings and orchids flowered high in the forest canopy. The paddy-bird drank at temple ponds and nested with crows in tamarind trees. Rocks sparkled with sapphires and emeralds. Dragon lizards sucked on eggs laid in nests of pink sand. Men recounted legends of gods and spirits and the histories of their ancestors. Black-eyed girls sat under the scented boughs of the 'Queen of the Night' and told the sad story of a princess who fell in love with the sun. It deserted her; she killed herself, but from the place where her body fell grew a tree. It sheds its flowers each morning, said to be unable to bear the sight of the sun.

The gods forgot Mannar and it fell from grace. Now the turtle beaches have been usurped. Neither snow nor leopard visits the foothills of its solitary peak. Waterfalls plunge into dead rivers that flow into polluted estuaries. Coral, blasted from the reefs, lies bleached among oil that has come ashore. Rubber and frankincense are no longer tapped. Ebony, teak and mahogany have been stripped from forests and the ironwood tree stands as sole protector from erosion. The elephant is almost extinct, hunted for its tusks, which are sold as trinkets in bazaars. Monkeys pick through the garbage which is piled high in the streets. Bee-eaters and orchids are so rare that it is a privilege to catch sight of them. The pink-headed duck and most of its kind have been hunted to extinction and the 'immortal' crow is no longer accompanied by the paddy-bird. The ancient cities lie in ruins, their water tanks cracked and dry. The gemstones have all been mined. Starvation, previously unknown, has found its way into country and city. In dusty squares would-be politicians spout oratory that sends men delirious with dreams. The black-eyed girls have lost their childhood and with it the story of the 'Queen of the Night'. They stand in sunless alleys and sell themselves to passers-by.

Sir Alexander Haye: television personality, zoologist, chairman of wildlife conservation committees, patron of London Zoo. Alexander was adored by the audiences of his natural history programmes, which were syndicated around the world. His face was known and appeared on the covers of books. In a quiet way he was famous. Those who recognised him were always surprised by his presence, for nothing quite matched his image on screen. He was a little bigger, a little sharper, a little more colourful than they had imagined – like a beam of light that passes through a prism and fractures into a rainbow. There was an aura of wellbeing about Alexander, as if little had really ever gone wrong for him and foreseeably little would. Only his voice was recognisably the same. He was married to Olivia and together they made a glamorous couple. It was a fact that they were unhappy, although Olivia was always at his side.

Together they flew to Mannar for several meetings with its President and members of its House of Representatives, and to prepare for filming rare wildlife on the island. It was to be a series of films to bring solace to his viewers, showing them that there were still remote areas of the world where large mammals roamed free and were breeding productively. The President hoped that Mannar would be reinstated on celluloid to its former glory as a 'Garden of Eden'. He hoped that the film would bring attention to his forgotten dominion, a return of tourism and a renewal of both financial and humanitarian aid.

As corruption amongst politicians had become rife, most rich, important countries in the world had ceased to consider Mannar, under its present government, to be worthy of aid. As Alexander outlined his intentions for his film, the President could see that it might stimulate exactly the foreign resources that he needed to remain in power.

Nothing was said directly to Alexander about terrorism; no politician of the ruling party spoke openly about the growing revolt on the island. It was important, in order to maintain power, not to admit that Mannar was bubbling and erupting like boiling mud, fired by poverty and despair. Those who governed had no commitment to anyone other than themselves. It was a fact that as many gems as were mined earned nothing for the island, but sat uncut in the claustrophobic dark of safe-deposit boxes around the world, waiting to be released, to sparkle in a gem dealer's eye before being locked away again, within the vaults of the rich.

This eruption was unstoppable and the population of the island was trapped in the uneasy prelude of outrage countered by atrocity, of violence suppressed only by more violence.

The assistance and protection of the army were offered to Alexander and his film crew. The President prided himself on still having control of the army. They would have access to vehicles and helicopters that were in short supply, since so many had been captured or destroyed by 'these scoundrels', as the President described them. Late one night, after a long and trying meeting to finalise arrangements, whilst sharing a bottle of Cognac and some Cuban cigars Alexander had given to the President, the magnanimous offer of a gift of a baby elephant to London Zoo was made.

It was a bribe. Alexander knew. He accepted. The acquisition of one of these rare creatures would be just the publicity he required for his film and be good for the zoo.

Mass tourism and even exclusive safaris to wildlife and game reserves were a thing of the past. So many parts of the world rich in wild animals were situated in areas that had through famine, war and terrorism become too dangerous to visit. From these reserves animals were looted for any part of their bodies that could be sold to raise money for arms. They became larders for the hungry and those beasts that were deemed worthless became target practice for the disaffected. They languished beneath a bureaucracy that ate up most of their budgets. Representatives sent abroad to conferences on environmental issues misused spending money that their impoverished countries could not afford. 'Save the fragile planet' had become the tawdry banner beneath which they marched as they met in a merry-go-round of international cities.

Zoos were once again as popular as they had been when first built. They had breeding programmes for rare and near-extinct species and much-publicised projects for their return to the wild, but these were a sop to visitors. Their real purpose was to entertain. The elephant would be a crowd-puller. Its rarity, and thus its value to Mannar as a bargaining chip or bribe, meant that although a mother and her baby were to be selected they were to be separated. Only the baby would be transported to London.

The President smiled, satisfied that Alexander's film and his acceptance of the elephant would provide for his future. His exile had been long planned, but greed and vanity made him hang on for more handouts with which to gild his retirement.

Before Alexander returned to London to negotiate worldwide distribution with the company that was backing his film, all that was left to do was to persuade his twin brother Max, who lived on the island, to travel up to hill country and oversee the walking of the chosen mother and baby elephant down to the airport.

For the first time since he had come to live on Mannar Max felt the acute sensation of cold in a tropical climate. A ride in a military helicopter from an army station near the coast up to hill country left him numb and bewildered as he stood alone on a circle of bald red mud in a drizzle of rain. Above him rotor blades fanned with a mosquito's high whine. In the whirlwind of deafening noise he felt a moment of panic and raised his hands above his head, as if to grasp at a lifeline that would winch him back on to the helicopter. Seen from the air, Max gave only the appearance of waving absurdly at the departing aircraft.

He heard laughter from one side of the clearing. Children, huddled together under a sheet of blue and orange polythene, leapt up and scrambled away like a Chinese paper dragon. There was not a sound after they left. He pulled a typewitten piece of paper from his pocket; a sort of itinerary. It said: 'Transport waiting at military helicopter station.'

A dilapidated Toyota Landcruiser, parked some yards away beneath an open shelter roofed in corrugated iron, started up its engine. Max let out an audible breath of resignation, picked up his small suitcase, which was splattered with mud, and walked towards the waiting vehicle.

For some ten miles he was driven along slippery unmetalled service roads that crisscrossed tea estates. It was a monotonous landscape of undulating hills, closely terraced and densely planted with tea bushes. Occasionally he saw what resembled a cantonment, workers' accommodation, like houses of cards strung along muddy strips, stranded in an ocean of shiny green leaves.

Finally, a small native procession came into view ahead, travelling on foot at elephant pace. They looked solemn and self-absorbed like pilgrims on route to a religious festival. Max stepped down from the army vehicle and climbed up into the open-sided cab of a waiting truck. It was painted with pale camouflage patterns, over which were stencilled the words 'Department for the Conservation of Mannar Island Wildlife' and underneath, 'Save our Elephants'. The back was loaded with an assortment of equipment and provisions for men to make camp at night, beside the mother elephant and her baby.

Siri, the driver, sat at the wheel huddled in a dirty blanket. A brown knitted balaclava covered his head, pierced only by the whiteness of his eyes and a glistening of catarrh that dribbled from his nose. Without introduction he began to complain bitterly about the cold in the hills. He said he was a man of the hot plains and had worked in the only game reserve that the island possessed, taking tourists out in Jeeps in pursuit of vanishing wildlife.

Since a series of terrorist bombings of luxury hotels and an extended drought, few visitors came to the island or the reserve. Now at the reserve they were more likely to come upon the desiccated remains of a water buffalo, or a mange-ridden bear, than the once common herds of elephant. Only dirty white pariah kites and black jungle crows seemed to thrive, flocking around parched beasts who had given up their search for water. Siri, too, had joined the scavengers, for there were skins and ivory to profit from.

Exhaust fumes seeped up through the floor of the lorry, insinuating their poisonous vapours into the lungs of the two men. Max's head ached. With each judder of the vehicle over the ill-made road he felt a jangled pain, as if his brain had shrunk and was rolling and bruising against the inside of his skull. His discomfort was aggravated by Siri, who kept up a high-pitched, nasal monologue of such tedium that even his frequent curses came as relief. The lorry, which he drove mostly in third gear, repeatedly stalled. At every corner it slid towards a precipitous drop at the side of the road, causing Max's heart as well as his brain to lurch.

Siri did not associate with the mahouts. He tended to hang about on the fringes drinking a coarse brew of palm alcohol, with excuses that it was a remedy for the cold he suffered. This he blamed on the hill climate. He snivelled and coughed, dragged phlegm from his lungs and spat it out of the window of the cab.

An unremitting gloom settled on Max at the prospect of having to spend time in the close company of this man. The mist did not lift for the entire day but sat dankly, muffling sounds of the tea pluckers as they worked the terraces on either side of the road.

Max leant out of the cab of the lorry and looked back to where the mother elephant walked with her baby at her flank. The solemn progress of the animals, innocent of the purpose of their journey, saddened him. He longed to cry out to them, a warning call, especially a warning about himself. 'Beware ... beware,' he whispered, but they had been taught to trust men. He didn't know their language, was mute in their presence, overwhelmed by a powerlessness that he had not experienced for years.

'Two peas in a pod.' Words used by the midwife attendant at Max and Alexander's birth. 'Identical twins.' Part of a whole, less than a whole, different from one another yet to all the world the same. They grew up together and during that time a silken thread had woven itself through those years of childhood, backwards and forwards, to and fro. Max felt its constraints, remembered their shared terror at the sight of a photograph of Siamese twins joined at the head. He loved Alexander but felt cursed by that love, yet he was powerfully drawn to his own reflection. Max had travelled halfway round the world in order to put distance between himself and Alexander. Yet like the story of the ape in the Jardin des Plantes in Paris, who, after months of coaxing by a scientist, produced the first drawing by an animal: the sketch showed the bars of the poor creature's cage. It had only taken one call from Alexander for Max's help in this mission and years and distance and independence vaporised. A fine taut wire extended between them. Alexander had twitched the thread. Max responded.

Max, overwhelmed by uncertainties about what he was doing, became increasingly unhappy about the outcome of this journey and the motives of his brother.

Any understanding of what had led him agree to help Alexander became as nebulous as the mist around him. He settled into a malaise whose most punishing symptom were these thoughts hissing away like tinnitus inside his head. Mist and cloud merged together, obscuring the road in front of them. The lorry bore on unsteadily through a lingering abstraction of vapour. Max closed his eyes and felt the full force of the painful pulse within his brain.

That night he spent in comfort as guest of one of the island's notables. A former politician, now manager of a large government tea estate, Vinny Peralta lived with his family in an old planter's bungalow. Roofed in red corrugated iron, it perched in the hills. A flamboyant, corpulent man, Vinny's baggy trousers were supported by coloured silk braces, pulling them halfway up his chest so that the fly fastening sat on top of his belly.

The evening started with tumblers filled to the brim with whisky and soda, accompanied by sweetmeats, which his host seized in handfuls with his small pudgy fingers and swallowed in single gulps. The two men sat out on the large veranda. Below them rivers of mist rolled down hillsides and flowed through valleys like flash floods. Peaks of ultramarine were slowly isolated from one another and the last cries of birds echoed across the chill white turbulence. Max felt a tug of anxiety as a pale sun extended its last rays across the landscape, clutching on to what remained of day, then lost its grip and seemingly fell into a limitless lake of night.

From the kitchens came sweet and spicy smells of a feast being prepared. Delicacy after delicacy was served by the shy wife, daughters and servants of his host. Hospitality and respect pressed down upon Max. He felt unaccountably out of control. Events had taken on a dreamlike quality from which he stood aloof. Alexander was beside him again. Max, unable to disentangle himself from the reality of what was happening, sat back, an onlooker.

After the women retired he was left alone with his host sipping a 'nightcap'. A roaring wood fire blazed up the chimney, sucking damp night from the dimly lit room. It resembled an Edwardian parlour, with large heavy furniture swathed in plush materials. The unfamiliar chill in the air, the gilded warmth of the fire on his face, made Max feel momentarily sentimental for the temperate climate he had left behind so long ago. He had a fleeting memory of Alexander standing beside him, his pale hair shining in the firelight, both of them transfixed as they watched a black beetle, marooned on a log, struggle to escape from the heat of the fire. The closer the flames came the more frenzied the beetle got, until Max could bear it no longer and leant forward and rescued the creature. Alexander leapt up and punched his twin, winding him, claiming that it was his experiment and it had been ruined. Max dropped the beetle; it was lost to some corner of the room. He felt a stinging disappointment with himself that he had been unable to sit back and watch the insect go to its fate.

There was the sound of a car, footsteps on the veranda outside, a rush of night air as another guest was shown into the room by a manservant. Vinny Peralta rose up from his chair and stood slightly unsteadily on his feet to welcome his guest, just arrived from the capital.

'J. D. Silva.' Max shook his hand. 'Call me Jaydee.' He was younger and marginally fitter than his host and dressed in a blazer and a club tie. He was an important banker and economic adviser to the President. His presence had been anticipated all evening.

'So sorry to be late . . . apologise to your wife about dinner . . . what a blessed relief to be here,' he said as he sank down into a chair, raised his hand and snapped his fingers behind his ear. The elderly manservant stepped forward from where he had been dozing in an unlit passage.

'Brandy and soda, boy.' Jaydee flopped his oiled black hair back on to a starched white antimacassar.

'You don't know what a charmed life you lead up here. How I envy you. Away from the hurly-burly of city life.' He sighed ostentatiously. In his voice Max heard both superiority and anxiety to establish his status in their company.

'Yes, speaking for myself, I am content,' replied his host. Although attentive to his guest, after a fine dinner and some alcohol, Vinny was not on his mettle and in other circumstances would have slipped into a drowsy sleep until wakened by his wife and sent to bed. As he sat back in his chair he had to fight to stay awake.

Jaydee, drink in hand, addressed Max. 'Met your brother, Sir Alexander, today. Dinner with the President, a grand affair.'

Vinny was suitably impressed and tried to lean forward in his chair, clinging to the arm for support. With a look of confusion on his face, a plea for rescue, he turned to Max.

'They are gossiping all the time. Talking about this one, talking about that one, talking about another one.' Vinny looked straight at Max, trying to imply inside knowledge.

'Fine man, your brother, fine man. This film of his'll do wonders for us.'

Suddenly Max felt utterly manipulated. He wanted to flee from the overheated claustrophobia of this parlour, join the mahouts outside around their camp fire and breathe in the smell of elephants and chilled air. He was angry at Alexander for his misguided vanity in wanting a baby elephant as publicity for his film. Angrier still at his own acquiescent passivity. Sickened with himself, he listened silently to the two men.

The conversation turned to the increasing outbreaks of violence and lawlessness, the failure of even the most basic infrastructure. Since the island's economy had slumped, sections of the unemployed and undernourished populace had turned to sporadic acts of terrorism as the only solution to their plight.

'Insignificant . . . factional infighting for control of resources. Families settling old scores, over land rights. This sort of thing has been happening for generations and will go on after we're all long dead.' Jaydee was now in full flow, the large star sapphire in his tiepin glinting in the firelight. Vinny was lapping up his arguments, they were so much what he wanted to hear. Max felt even more uneasy and faintly sick. That afternoon he had heard a rumour amongst the elephant party of a massacre of half the adult men of a small community a few miles from the capital. A cache of imported arms and ammunition had been discovered. The speculation was that the violence had the support of an outside power. An avaricious coloniser was back, sitting on the sidelines, like a vulture waiting for enough carnage to take place before coming in to pick the flesh from the bones.

'Our infrastructure's sound enough. Why, just look at the bank.'

'But the bureaucracy . . .' interrupted Max.

'That's *your* legacy, old chap.' Both men turned and smiled at Max.

'Frankly, I'll admit it's a problem,' said Jaydee. 'With the universities closed for the last two years our intake of graduates at the bank has been nil. Those we had are bleeding away as we speak. We can't restructure.'

'You can see, changes are not anything to the good, water situation is so bad,' muttered Vinny. Having lost the direction of the conversation, he drifted off to sleep.

'Isn't it that nepotism . . . ?' Max immediately wished

that he had not been so naïve as to mention the word, but it was true that high-born families clung on to every senior position in the government. Every post of any significance was filled by a relation or intimate of the regime.

'What I meant to say was, graduates . . .' He tailed off, seeing the hardening expression on Jaydee's face.

Nepotism was not a word that was used openly, it suggested injustice; those in government preferred to regard this as a benevolent regime. The fact was, it was almost impossible for an islander to get a decision on any matter concerning his human rights or his land rights. Such a request presented a man with the prospect of waiting a lifetime for an outcome.

'Troublemakers,' interjected Jaydee in a bellicose tone, the drink having given a liverish turn to his mood.

'I agree with you one hundred per cent,' said Vinny, hoping to pacify his important guest.

The old night servant passed between them like a feather blown across the room, stacked wood on the fire, refilled all their glasses, was gone. Max was aware that the two men had become uncomfortable with him, Jaydee leant forward in his chair and looked steadily at Max. A man drunk but charmed by his own eloquence.

'What you have to realise is that Mannar islanders are indolent, it's their nature. Why work . . .? There's fruit on the trees, water in rivers and game in the forests. Life's easy. No one really starves.' He turned to their host.

'Look at this estate. Workers housed, primary education, medical care, that speaks tremendously for the ethos of our government.' The two men nodded with complicit satisfaction.

'Now to be frank with you, old chap,' he leant even further forward and lowered his voice to a conspiratorial level, 'I have to admit that this minority dissent is a bit of a problem. But we've given carte blanche to the police and the army. They can use whatever means they consider necessary to root out these scallywags.'

'Disaffected intellectuals. The universities are a breeding ground, that's why we've closed 'em down.' Their host pushed his thumbs behind his braces and yawned.

Max listened uneasily to what these men had to say. He, like most of the people of Mannar, was largely uninformed, except by hearsay. No mention was made in the press or on television of incidents. Warnings that some wariness should be exercised went unheeded. Here he had constructed for himself a model of perfection: his rocky outcrop just offshore, a circle of paradise, of which he was master. To have looked into the political and human abyss would have been to eat of the fruit of the Tree of Knowledge, so he hid amongst its branches and surveyed only the beauty at its feet.

Overnight the weather improved. Max woke, his head reeling from the alcohol he had drunk the night before. He got up and sleepwalked across the unfamiliar room, then opened the window to breathe. Early morning mist clad the land and above it rose a pale disc of sun. He breathed in again. Through blurred eyes he turned away from the light and looked down on sloping acres of neatly tended tea bushes. Lush shiny leaves sparkled with dew that slithered and shimmered like quicksilver under the morning sun. He squinted and imagined those camellias in full waxy flower, breaking open their spiral white buds to the bright air. Then a chattering multitude of brown fingers flew over the plants and all that remained were infertile plucked shrubs.

Max had to come to hate his nightly stops; as the afternoon sun lowered and the countryside recovered from the noonday glare, he dreaded the prospect. Alexander had taken control. There were an elephant, her baby, a string of men, an itinerary that was seemingly impossible to defy, a genial welcome waiting for him from his next host. Max found himself unreasonably irritated by excessive hospitality. Their desire for gossip and news that he was unable to provide. A spurious belief that with such a famous brother he must be at the centre of things. Still he sat in their midst and continued the charade, half listening to their sombre warnings about the unrest on the island. He convinced himself that not to have played on would have been churlish. He felt his deception most acutely when he remembered that he had been welcomed on this island. Each night as time approached to make camp he longed only to be able to return to his former serenity, to that patch of land that belonged to him.

Max's qualms about delivering the baby elephant to

the airport increased. He grew sadder at the utter futility of the whole idea and his part in it. Sending a single member of an almost extinct species to a life of solitary confinement seemed so absurd that he felt there must be someone who could understand the wantonness. At night, as he lay in bed, he was plagued by thoughts that he should intervene. Several times he vowed to leave the procession, go to the President, at the very least to plead the case for the mother elephant, but his good intentions evaporated with the dawn. As he tossed and turned he felt a gross and passive figure.

Increasingly he refused after-dinner drinks with his particular host for that night with excuses that he had to be up by dawn to see the elephants and the men set out. Everyone, he knew, with the exception of Siri, was entirely capable, and often he woke to the cries of the mahouts signalling that they were about to set out on the next day's walk. Elephants and men left punctually every morning just after dawn.

On reaching the warmer foothills Max felt a certain relief. The claustrophobia of chill evenings on tea plantations was behind him. He spent a night with an ex-army officer, a tall, lean, languorous man with a self-confident manner.

'It's an old story, the story of this place; we've seen models for it time and time again, but we believed it would not happen to us. Meanwhile, we've neglected the seeds of ferment. It's too late. You will see. We are small but because we are small the kernel will split itself apart ferociously. We have nothing to offer those who are disaffected. We have ignored our problems, denied their existence. No one from the capital will venture out. They don't want to see or hear what is going on.' The officer paused. 'Fat-cat politicians,' he muttered to himself bitterly. 'They treated us as if we were there to provide joyrides in our helicopters or put on a show to aid their self-aggrandisement.'

Max felt a twinge of guilt as he remembered the military helicopter that had transported him to the beginning of his journey with the elephants. He looked about the room. It was sparse and ordered. Only the minimum of furniture and almost no personal objects. Curiously, the walls were crisscrossed by brown-stained slats of wood, giving the impression of a mock-Tudor hunting lodge. Between, the divisions were crammed with photographs, old engravings and aquatints, all in identical narrow black frames. Family, school, army, the man's whole life was catalogued. Passing his gaze across the pictures, Max felt he was flicking through an old book in which the last few pages remained uncut, still holding the secret of what was to happen at the end.

There were photographs of sportsmen in sola topis and tweed knickerbockers standing smugly behind dead buffalo. Stags held up by their antlers by trackers to give a better photograph. The officer kneeling by a dead leopard, its head lolling; a Jack Russell dog perched on its back. Pictures of men in front of their camps in the hills, in the foreground their catches of fish; colossal taimen and lenok dangling from wires with gasping mouths and jagged teeth.

The officer saw Max's interest and smiled to himself.

'Those were the days. Lost for ever, I am sorry to say.' At this acquiescence to his curiosity Max looked harder. At the Tent Club members on horseback, spears in hand after successful pig-sticking, marshalled behind a huge boar stretched over a wooden barrel. Its head was raised by a stave driven up through its throat, and its tiny eyes and ears and tusks pointed unnaturally at the sky. Pairs of leashed and hooded cheetah were sitting on the backs of country carts, waiting to run down deer and lap their blood. Pictures of polo teams, regattas and gymkhanas. The group photograph dominated.

Above these were ranged trophies: stuffed heads of ibex, skulls with gaping eye sockets and the mammoth ridged horns of markhor and sharpoo. Over the mantel-piece hung a huge black and white reproduction of *The Stag at Bay* by Landseer. Max found himself intimidated by these images of animals with terrified eyes, wary of his host and his beguiling mildness of manner.

It was dusk outside; already the frogs had begun their chorus and the mosquitoes were rising in battalions from coir swamps. The man got up, as if to call to a servant, but hesitated and slowly began to unfold the slatted wooden shutters from within. 'Come, I have something to show you.' As they passed along an enclosed veranda he continued to fasten and bolt shutters until they reached a room at the end, a bedroom, his room. Dull and scant in its interior except for one extraordinary sight. A movement led Max to realise that there was something alive in the room. At the foot of the officer's bed stood a hooded falcon. She swivelled her head through 180 degrees, from where she had been resting her beak at the back of her neck, and ruffled her feathers. 'This is Angel.' The officer crossed the room, knelt down and removed the tiny cockaded embroidered hood from the falcon's head. She looked at Max with her hard golden eye from beneath her straight feathered brow. 'May I?' Max leant forward and ran the back of his hand down her feathered breast. She stood proudly, turning her head with sudden jerks, so that if you blinked you could not be quite certain whether she had moved at all so absolutely still was she between each turn. A huntress sighting her prey. The officer replaced the hood over the bird's head and she puffed her feathers and lowered herself as if to tilt off the perch, but then settled into her blind captivity.

They returned to the sitting room. The officer put a match to the fire laid in the grate. It smouldered and hissed and sung as the heat of the flames scorched the wood.

'Please, please sit down.' Max sat and watched a small gecko scamper from its hiding place.

'Last night the lights went. I am fortunate in that I have my own generator.' Still standing with his back to the windows, he paused for some seconds and looked solemnly at Max.

'I heard the silence.' Max watched as the gecko hid behind a sepia photograph of three children in sailor suits. 'I got up, took out my pistol, went to look for my man, but I did not call out. In the dark I listened to the silence.' He paused thoughtfully, then leant forward and squashed a small black fruit fly that was crawling around the rim of his starched cuff.

'It's a silence that I know from years of military service. Different, charged. It exists when all about seems absolutely normal; heightened by the breath of a breeze through jungle or the slightest flick of one palm frond against another. The silence that surrounds a group of sleeping leopards in a tree, where no beast dares to call out for fear of discovery but slips away into jungle. When even the lizard retracts its tongue and seals its jaws. Fear and numbness are that silence . . . I am familiar with it . . . I'm a professional . . . I understand the effects on the body. Out on patrol I could always tell how long a man would survive by his reaction to silence.'

He crossed the room, turned casually to Max and raised a bottle of whisky that was in his hand. Max nodded. He took up a glass from a side table, where he filled it with whisky and water, lifted the lid of an ice bucket, paused and replaced the lid. 'No ice . . . not tonight, I'm sorry,' he paused. 'Well, as I said, last night I was woken by silence.' Max was rigid, as tight as the weave of the rattan chair on which he sat. Outside frogs chorused. He nodded his thanks to the officer as he was handed his drink and waited for him to continue.

'I walked out on to the pyal. Even the frogs had dulled their song.' Both men sipped at their drinks. There was a clatter on the roof overhead. A palm civet thundered across and slid down a wooden post of the veranda outside.

'The smell of burning rubber streamed towards me. I let off a bullet into the dark. It popped into the night. Broke the silence. I listened to a struggle in the brush at the boundary of my property. Let off another, and another, before I went down.' He paused. 'I found my man, hands and feet bound. He lay beside my vehicle. The tyres had been removed from the wheels. One hung round his neck and his body rested on the others. They were smouldering. The inner edge had melted, but they had failed to catch fire. Not enough petrol. So you find me without servants and my man. He lies scarred in the room beside yours. His crime, my crime? We were in the army.'

This was further from the path than Max had wanted to stray. Suddenly he longed for the inanity of the conversations that he had listened to for the last few days. Their blindness to the unrest on the island; the lack of political will even to admit to these problems, let alone attempt to deal with them. His unease was compounded by this man's calm acceptance of the atrocity that had occurred. He wanted to flee, but outside stood the mother elephant and her baby, like some monumental anchorage.

'All the village will have heard of this incident. By

attacking me they need do no more; they will not return. For you see, now everyone is afraid. No one will speak. No one will tell. But every man, woman and child hereabouts understands.'

Max finished his drink. Admiration for the officer's tranquillity wheedled its way inside him like a shaft of light through the canopy of fear that shaded him. The gecko re-emerged from behind the picture frame and angled its way up the wall behind him in pursuit of an insect. It let out a small cry like a bird, and scuttled into a crevice.

That night Max slept badly. The tinnitus of betrayal hissed in his ears. Outside the mahouts were watchful about a smouldering fire. Once the mother elephant trumpeted a warning at the garrulous night.

On the coastal plain the temperature rose. Listening to Siri clearing his lungs above the noise of the exhausted, dragging engine, juddering in low gear, Max decided to abandon the lorry and travel with the elephant procession. The mother and her baby were so mild and gentle they seemed to affect everyone who walked with them. At the sight of the elephants, children emerged from emerald green jungle chattering with excitement, leaping with delight. They were like the clouds of yellow butterflies that fluttered in rays of sunlight along the roads, vanishing as suddenly and magically as they had arrived to another patch of sun where they would repeat their joyous dance.

Siri, bored by the slowness of the procession, took advantage of each new situation. He was unable to resist a tavern, where those who frequented it were immediately his best friends or sparring partners.

As the quantity of distilled spirit he consumed increased he seemed to acquire relations, friends, or acquaintances of friends and relations. There was always someone to offer him shade and a drink at whatever place he had slyly decided to break down.

On returning to the truck Siri was invariably drunk. Then he drove at frenzied speed, slicing through the chaotic late afternoon traffic in order to get to the next camp. He turned into a man possessed, stamping on the accelerator and the brake alternately without changing gear, as the clutch teeth were torn off between grinding plates.

Alcohol set loose in him a hidden malice towards man and beast that he did not appear to harbour at other times. It compelled him to direct his vehicle straight at any creature that lay in his path. If the road was empty he would lunge towards a sleeping dog curled up on the dusty track beside the edge of the tarmac, as if it were a marauding jackal, causing it to yelp in fright and flee before its head or hindquarters were bruised by his tyres. He'd laugh out loud and press the horn continuously. The cab turned into a fairground switchback ride, where the man who had power over the controls had lost his sanity. He felt a particular superiority over bullock carts. To him they were an inferior form of transport and a

26

target for abuse. He would sound the horn, curse and gesticulate at innocent men and their cattle as if it was his dearest wish to see both relegated to a lesser highway.

On the afternoon after they had made camp with the officer, Siri was particularly belligerent and drove straight towards a line of boulders that had been placed across half the road. The area was being used by some fishermen to sort their nets. A thud on the front of the truck caused him to lose control. He veered off to one side, heading straight for some children playing around a banana stall. He narrowly missed them, but shattered the front of the truck against a palm tree. The radiator cracked and hissed water on to the dust. Max, who had been walking with the elephant party, came upon Siri surrounded by a crowd of threatening men and women.

Their violent reaction to this incident had been inflamed by a visit from the police at daybreak. Alleging that the villagers were hiding arms and terrorists, they had brutally searched each dwelling. In frustration at finding nothing, they had arrested several young men and taken them away in their jeeps for detention and torture. Throughout the day the villagers had tried to restore the wanton damage to their peaceful lives. Loss of their sons to internment, without any recourse to justice, had left them in a state of angry frustration. Siri's drunken accident had been all that they needed to push them further than they would ever have considered possible.

Max approached the terrified, inarticulate man surrounded by a mob seeking revenge for their despair. He felt a dangerous charge in the air. With all the authority he could muster he went forward into their midst and publicly admonished Siri for his behaviour. He sacked him, relieved, at last, to be free of the man. This defused the anger of the crowd. Women and children went to see the elephant party and a mechanic was sent for to repair the lorry. From then on Max took over the driving. He dropped Siri at their next night stop, where he left him to find his own way back to the reserve.

Max's attachment to the mother elephant and her baby deepened. It became a silken luxury to travel with them. The animals were taken to lakes and washed lovingly by their mahouts. There they would wallow, and tease, and play together. They sprayed trunks full of water over one another and all about them.

The local people, unfamiliar with elephants, came to watch. Grandfathers brought their grandchildren to sit on the banks and wade into the water. They retold old stories and myths about the elephants of their own childhood: of their longevity, their intelligence, of secret caverns that they had travelled to at night for salt. On the walls of these caverns, worn away by time, were undulating reliefs that were thought by some to be the telling of their history, from before man had lived on earth. Holy men had lived in these caves and translated these reliefs of sacred beasts to those who aspired to understand. The people of Mannar believed that a man who had reached an extreme state of self-denial and transcended his own bodily being could read and interpret the reliefs and obtain knowledge and understanding of the integral nature of the universe.

The holy men told of the elephants' precognition of their own impending death. Of their graveyards that were known only to the elders of the herds, to which they travelled, often weak and sick and decrepit with age, to die. Of ivory hunters who had searched all their lives for these places, just as men searched for gold, but had always been unrewarded. Of warriors who tamed the elephants and used them as mounts in battle. Of the bravery of the bulls. Of the sacred nature of the animal, which was known only from carvings on temples and photographs in books. Of the cruelty of the hunters, who would saw off the tusks from a half-dead animal, an exploded bullet in its brain, while the herd looked on, maddened with rage, or scattered in terror. Of the fortunes made out of carving and selling trinkets to a world ravenous for creamy, polished ivory. Of the elephant's near extinction.

Max, always one step away from the men who were looking after the elephants, found that he longed now to be part of their camp. Each night, while he endured lavish hospitality, he smelt the smoke from their wood fire. He listened to the mahouts' chatter as they made camp with the elephant and her baby in their midst. He lay restlessly under his netted shroud, a kerosene lamp at his bedside, and outside a servant sleeping on the floor in case he might require something during the night. He felt imprisoned.

It was weeks since the mosquito had punctured his skin. Max had been quite unaware of it. She had merely been one of the hordes of biting insects that plagued the island at that time of year. Stagnant pools of water in the low-lying areas between the hills and the coast had been breeding disease faster than the coming change in season.

Day after day they passed through forest, drank at the foot of waterfalls, trudged through swamp-bordered villages. Max became increasingly attached to the mother elephant and her baby. He was ever more aware of the treachery that he was to be party to when they reached their destination. As they walked she swung her trunk to and fro, clutching at passing vegetation and pushing it into her mouth. Her baby followed close to her flank.

Only once did the mother elephant refuse to go further. They were on a bullock-cart track between paddy fields and for no accountable reason she stopped. The mahouts warned that the day was inauspicious for travel and that the beast knew. Max was haunted by this and felt that the elephant had some precognition of what would happen if she went further. Whatever the reason, she would not move. Unable to deal with an immobile elephant and unwilling to confront the fates, Max decided that they should rest. He declined an offer to stay in the village with an excuse that the elephants were disturbed and that it was his duty to stay with them. He watched as the mother elephant tore up grass and turned it in the air with her trunk, sifting it in the wind. When formed into a ball, she gently lowered it and beat it against one of her forefeet to separate out the dust. This silent rhythmic task was repeated to a gentle swaying of her entire form. When the herbage was to her satisfaction she scooped it up in the curve of the tip of her trunk and pushed it into her mouth. Beside her, her baby copied her, inexpertly got dirt into his trunk and snorted several times before he abandoned his mimicry and went to suckle from his mother. From beside Max came a rumble from the mother elephant like the purring of some gigantic cat.

Mesmerised by the sounds and movements of the elephants, he lay all afternoon in his hammock unable to tell whether it was his own sweat or saturation humidity that so irritated his skin. Just before dusk swarms of insects rose from the surrounding stagnant water. He slept and woke after dark. Above him was a starry sky. Clear across the fields from the nearby village came the discordant noise of drums as a 'Devil Dance' was performed. A mahout came to Max with some food and asked if he would like to witness the rite. He declined. Mosquitoes sucked and bit. He pinched and squashed them between the close-worked holes of his mosquito net. The elephant stood with her baby beside her, caressing it with her trunk all night on the raised narrow track.

Just before daybreak the drums stopped and a morbidly depressed mother was freed of the bad spirits that had taken her over after the death of her son. Max looked out as the sun rose through his bloodstained net. There was no more trouble from the elephant. She walked steadily without incident all the way to the airport.

Two reporters, a television crew and some photographers from the Mannar Island Ministry of Information were waiting for them as they arrived at the tin shed where the animals were to be fed and watered before the flight. Mistaking Max for Alexander, they called out to him.

'Sir Alexander . . . a picture with the elephants?' Flashlights and the whirr of cameras unsettled the animals. Angered, Max called upon some soldiers who were standing on the sidelines to get rid of the press. Delighted to be invited to be officious, they started waving their guns and demanding identification. The journalists retreated under protest to the main airport building.

The heat was intolerable inside the metal shed and sweat from the bodies of the mahouts hardly left their pores before it dried in salty smears on their brown skin. Mother and baby fanned their ears backwards and forwards, causing a soft dry turbulence in the air. Max pulled a crumpled jacket and tie from his bag and put them on. He splashed some water over his face and around the back of his neck and smoothed back his hair with his wet hands. He felt ridiculous. The mother elephant stretched out her trunk towards him and the tip passed over his right ear. The skin on her forehead fluttered. She was calling with an almost inaudible rumbling sound. She eyed him from under her long, straggled lashes as she reached down for another bundle of hay and pushed it into her mouth. Hardly able to face himself or to bear the presence of the elephant, he turned and walked away towards the main airport building.

The Minister for the Environment, a member of the House of Representatives and several other dignitaries were assembled, drinking large glasses of whisky mixed with tepid soda water. Max joined them. The Superintendent of Reserves gave a lengthy, meandering speech on the need for global education about the conservation of rare breeds.

The member of the House of Representatives spoke of the former Commonwealth island's close links with the United Kingdom. Of how sending one of their precious elephants to London Zoo would create good will between the two countries, whose past and present had been so closely linked. Max thought of the lines of immigrants sitting on benches on the edge of compounds, outside foreign embassies, patiently waiting to be genetically screened before they were permitted even to visit their relatives for a holiday.

Max gave a short speech of thanks on his brother's behalf. Somehow courtesy was easy. He could do it without thinking. But action, of that he was incapable. 'Alexander ... Alexander ...', he exhaled the syllables to himself, but it was useless to intone his brother's name as if to share the responsibility. The fates of the elephants were now upon his own conscience. He had proved to his twin that he was up to the experiment. He had resisted his urge to rescue the beetle from fire. It had taken half a lifetime for Max to reach this point. Half a lifetime to realise that he had been right to snatch it from its fate. And half a lifetime to know that he had made an unforgivable error of judgement. There was still time; he could create a scene or better still give an interview. He was surrounded by journalists. There was the television crew, one of them would want the story and he had access. They all knew his brother's face and thus his own. He could even be Alexander, most of them already thought that he was. Stand up, say it was all a mistake, refuse the elephant. He took a drink from the tray that was thrust in front of him. He swallowed the glass of whisky in one gulp and then put his hand out for another, in a vapid attempt to alleviate his self-despair.

Max quickly became slightly drunk and had to sit down. He looked about him, overwhelmed by the fact that no one else in this overcrowded room had grasped the pointlessness of sending a solitary male animal to its inevitable extinction. Glasses were refilled again and again while they waited for the baby elephant to be pre-pared for take-off. Everybody was grinning with pride through the heat and alcohol. Their elephant had got its exit visa cleared, a certificate of good health, its passport to the First World. They thought they understood. The television newsreel, the front-page coverage in the next day's papers, would give hope. Their baby was travelling to a better life.

Max was approached by the Minister for the Environment, a seedy-looking man.

'Congratulations, old chap.'

'Old chap. Old boy,' murmured Max to himself, reminded of the tea estate manager and the banker he had stayed with in the hills. He didn't stand up.

The Minister leant forward over Max, slopping some of the drink from his glass on to the arm of the sofa, and continued to talk at him. Max's thoughts had become quite incoherent. He stuttered what passed as a response.

Lowering his voice and leaning even further forward, the Minister whispered conspiratorially, 'President's giving a little party at his residence tonight, asked if you would attend, Sir Alexander being unavailable?'

At other times in his life Max might have reacted to the implied suggestion that he was second choice, but pulling himself out of his semi-inebriated daze he saw in this an opportunity to muster an excuse. It was, after all, Alexander whom the President wanted. What was Max Haye to him? At best a curiosity, at worst another lotus-eater. He stood up and, struggling to hang on to his presence of mind, rather formally composed a slurred response.

'Please convey to the President my gratitude for his unexpected invitation. But, tell him sadly I cannot attend. I've been travelling for weeks and it is imperative I return home to make preparations before Sir Alexander and his party arrive after filming the elephants at the reserve.'

Max chuckled to himself at the idiocy of this statement and its laboured delivery, but the pompous man in front of him seemed entirely satisfied.

'Can I get you another drink, my friend?' he said and without pausing for a reply was snapping his fingers and yelling, 'Boy, boy, over here. Boy, another whisky for Sir Alexander's brother.'

Max sank back down on to the sofa. His half-empty glass was removed from his hand and a full one put in its place. His mind lost its grip on the exchange, wandered and latched on to the word 'environment'. He couldn't remember whether he had ever known what the word meant. Less could he understand why it had come to be so well used that government ministries were set up in its name. Perhaps the loose meaning of the word enabled almost anything to be brought in under its umbrella. Syllables chased one another inside his head. En-vir-on-ment con-ser-va-tion looped themselves around his thoughts like barbed wire. He stared, glazed eyed, up into the face of the man in front of him. A flashlight exploded, and in the violet afterblaze the Minister's face cracked and sagged. It looked like the cardboard of the favelas of South America and the slums of all Asia. His breath stank of the sewers of that rich old world to which he longed to belong. Max blinked and turned away, making confused excuses that he must leave immediately to see the elephant on to the aeroplane.

He entered the shed just as the small elephant, soft furred, walked meekly into an iron crate. It was raised on a fork-lift, dragged out across the tarmac behind a tractor, and loaded into the bowels of the plane. The mother stood by tossing hay into the air, filling the filtered sunlight with clouds of dust. Max walked out on to the sweltering tarmac. The sky was turning grey and a combination of the smell of jet fuel and saturation humidity pressed hard into his lungs. Government officials, the Superintendent of Reserves and the press milled about drunkenly in the simmering heat, each uncertain about quite what the formalities were, and who should stand where. Max found his way to the end of the line. He staggered slightly as he was passed from hand to hand, until he was placed in a position that was thought to be equivalent to his status on this occasion. He stood, shoulders sagging, swaying slightly, his face red and sweating with heat and drink, a grieved and troubled figure.

Involuntarily he watched. A man with yellow table tennis bats led the jet out of its parking bay. It waited, engines charged, for the signal from the control tower for take-off. All clear. It started to taxi along the runway and lift into the sky when there was a terrible commotion. Out of the open doors of the hangar charged the mother elephant, ears flapping, a chain dragging from one of her ankles, making sparks as it jangled over stones. She came directly towards the party of men still rooted to the tarmac. The Superintendent of

Reserves fled. The others huddled behind an expanding aluminium stepladder. Max did not move from the spot as the distressed elephant ran past him, trunk raised, ears flapping, trumpeting screams that were drowned by the noise of the jet engines as the aircraft reached the end of the runway and lifted off.

It was several hours before they recaptured the mother elephant. She stopped all traffic through the airport for the remainder of that day. Air traffic control watched her on its computer equipment as she flayed her trunk on a runway light. She refused to leave. She was tranquillised with a dart. Some monks came and declared her holy. Later she was painted with symbols to denote the spiritual deity that she represented and a makeshift temple was built around her.

She is still there. Her legs are chained together and she is fed on only the best herbage, which people donate. She stands at the airport. Travellers who have finally obtained their visas to their new life abroad come to worship her. They leave her gifts of marigold petals. Her baby resides at London Zoo.

Two

Max crossed to the empty airport building. The porters stood in a huddle by the door passing a cigarette between them. Since the elephant had closed the airport there had been no work. Max lowered his head and fixed his eyes on the dusty ground as they stood aside.

Thomas, his driver, was waiting. Max got into his car. Relief came as a sigh as the door slammed and Thomas turned the vehicle in the direction of home. He felt dizzy as the rusty old Pontiac heaved its chrome over potholes. They pulled out of the car park and on to the main road leading to the city.

The road was lined with coconut palms growing between the tall street lights. The concrete pillars had once been an object of civic pride. They had been erected a few years earlier and were the first public lighting in the entire country. The battle for supremacy over the palms had long been lost, and battered, dusty fronds draped themselves over the lamps, obscuring their symbolic statement of progress.

They passed over a rusting iron suspension bridge. As well as the road it carried a single-track railway across a polluted swamp that had once been a river in which families would bathe. Now no one was to be seen along its banks. The smooth flat stones where women used to do their washing were lapped by stinking sewage and chemical effluents from the city. Islands of sulphurous detergent foam remained eerily still as they flowed slackly towards the ocean.

The stream of traffic slowed, which was unusual at that time of day. Eventually Thomas was forced to stop. He turned off the engine so that the radiator would not boil over and they sat together in silence. The temperature inside the vehicle began to rise intolerably and the only air that came through its windows brought with it exhaust fumes and the wretched smell of the dead river. Max took out a packet of cigarettes and offered one to Thomas. He knew he never carried any of his own because his wife Maria disapproved of the habit. Together they smoked the cigarettes and filled the car with the odour of tobacco.

A turbulent pall of black smoke suddenly rose between the palm trees ahead of them. There was the sound of machine-gun fire. Just one rapid burst, then silence. Thomas started up the engine and tried to reverse. Max was jolted out of his melancholy inebriation. Thomas craned his neck in order to manoeuvre the car and turned round and looked at Max. A still second of fear passed between the two men.

At that moment, Max remembered the army officer and his man. His mind and body struggled to be free of the swaddling effects of alcohol, to release themselves with adrenalin. In confusion he opened the door of the car and tried to get out. Just as he placed his foot on the melting bitumen of the road a huge grey langur, accompanied by a gang of smaller monkeys, swung through the trees. They thundered down on to the bonnets and roofs of the cars. One clung momentarily to the front windscreen by the wipers and peered in at the two men. It contorted its face and bared its teeth in a leering grin before leaping away into the undergrowth.

A wild party of hooded men carrying staves and hatchets came running towards them, yelping and shouting as they passed either side of the line of vehicles ahead. At each they stopped and looked inside. Sometimes they shattered the windows and dragged men from their locked cars, kicking and screaming. Then hacked them down with their weapons. Drivers and passengers in the vehicles behind abandoned them, scattering on either side of the road. Some ran to the bridge and jumped into the river. Thomas jerked the bumper of the Pontiac into a car behind in his attempt to turn round and flee. Metal locked on metal. Black smoke swept along the line of traffic, filling the air with the smell of burning rubber. Max screamed at Thomas to get into the boot and hide, then he slid over the sticky leather upholstery into the driving seat.

Two men stopped, one either side of the car. They peered in through the windows. Jabbed muzzles of their repeating guns at the air like bayonets into flesh. Seeing the white face of what they assumed to be a tourist they passed on to the now empty line of cars behind. Max wrenched the car out of the jam, tearing off part of the other car's front bumper. It clattered behind them as he started to drive along the opposite side of the road towards the smoke. He reached the source of the fire, a bus, blocking the road, its front wheels lodged in an open concrete drain. Its tyres dropped heavy liquid dollops of flame into a putrid trickle of water underneath. Max put the Pontiac into reverse. From nowhere through the smoke came shadowy figures carrying short sawn logs. They threw them hurriedly into the drains at either end of the bus and vanished. Max jammed the gears into first. Crossed the rough bridge on to the dust. Turned and squinted up at the charred bus. Inside, like a glimpse into Hell, he could see blackened bodies. Some of the passengers were sitting bolt upright in their seats where the initial explosion had frozen them. One was still alive, running like a caged animal up and down the aisle between the seats, convulsing and twitching as his arms flailed about helplessly in a feeble attempt to put out his burning hair.

Max drove around the bus back on to the road, into a convoy of police and army vehicles. Muzzles of guns like hard metallic eyes peeped out from rips in their khaki canvas awnings. He was flagged down. Two soldiers took a desultory look inside and waved him on. He sped away as fast as he could towards the city, painfully aware of Thomas still huddled in airless torment in the boot of the car. He dared not risk stopping to release him so close to the insurgence.

Against the margins of the road festered the slums of a shanty town. Mangy dogs, scrawny hens and small grey pigs scavenged in open sewers and recycled detritus into survival. Transfixed, Max drove on past the neat low concrete bungalows of clerical workers and their families. Finally they reached the absurd building resembling a toy fort that was the railway station. Max turned off the road and parked under the shade of a mango tree; he got out to release Thomas. The man lay stupefied, huddled in the boot, exhausted by heat and fear. It took several ragged railway porters, in faded red coats, who had been standing by the station entrance, to assist him to uncurl his limbs and stagger to a bench under the mango tree. Still in shock, Max went over to a stall outside the station and collected two glasses of strong tea with milk and sugar. Released from their grip on the steering wheel, his hands trembled so much that he spilt half the hot liquid before reaching Thomas. The two men sipped at the brew. The inquisitive porters, who had heard that there had been trouble on the airport road, demanded to know what had happened.

An elderly, scrawny man, dressed only in a cotton

check dhoti which he had hitched up to half its length, pressed his face enquiringly close to Max, then he turned and raised his thin hurried voice towards a cluster of men a few yards away.

'Come, come, trouble on the airport road.' He wrung his brown stringy hands together and looked up beseechingly towards the heavens.

'What I ask myself is when will it all end? That is what I say.'

A brisk discussion started up between the men as they aired their grievances and voiced their individual suffering. Soon a considerable crowd gathered and exchanged their news. Their voices rose in a tumult of anger and horror. More and more strangers came closer and closer round Max and Thomas so that each might hear at first-hand of the incident.

'Tell, tell, what it is exactly that has been happening to you and your man? He is very afraid.'

The thin man had now taken on the role of interrogator for the crowd, who wanted to hear every detail of the incident. Max and Thomas were trapped. People were now taking sides, a growing irrationality was rising from their midst. The air simmered with their angry breath and the closeness of their bodies. It became intolerable and the two men fled to the sanctuary of their car, the crowd in pursuit. Max threw his hand out of the window and scattered some banknotes in front of the assembled porters who were blocking his exit. They fell on them like crows scrabbling in the dust and started fighting with

44

each other. The car spun its wheels in an attempt to get a grip in the dust and sped away.

They wove through the city, past the huge colonial government buildings. Their stuccoed walls glowed pink in the evening light and the sooty mould that festered there merged with the shadows. The buildings gave the appearance of having been freshly built of mother of pearl, hiding their decay.

Outside the House of Representatives a ragged huddle of men with placards were pleading with the government to come to the aid of their village.

The city's streets were bursting with noise and traffic. Children selling bruised garlands of jasmine and marigold flowers squeezed their tiny hands through the half-wound-up windows of the car. Beggars paraded their deformities at each halt. Garish multi-coloured political posters and plastic streamers dangled from every available post and wire. Walls and fences were smothered in a mishmash of symbol and print. At a crossroads a sandy dog lay on its side, its legs extended, its muzzle curled back into a smile. From its hindquarters a gush of shiny gelatinous blood spread across its coat. Such was the tumult, nobody stopped and a bicycle, avoiding an oncoming lorry, rode over one of its ears.

They passed the bus station, where queues of men waited for transport home, all seemingly dressed in identical white shirts and grey trousers, plastic flip-flops on their bare feet. Buddhist monks in saffron robes clung to their black umbrellas and their places of privilege at the front of these lines of workers. Max escaped the traffic by taking a detour through the embassy district, winding between European-style mansions that had once stood in acres of lawns on which gracious parties had been held. Here the first President of Mannar had been assassinated. The area was marred by shabby new breeze-block walls, automatic steel gates, and military men with security screens and electric eyes. Gardens had been divided and a new breed of fortified tomb-like buildings had been hurriedly constructed in windowless concrete. Rooftops covered in a chaos of communications equipment and satellite discs stared at the obsolete monuments of the past.

They turned out of the city through a wasteland of ambitious projects. There was a fish-freezing factory which had never had its ice plant constructed. Although the first catches had been delivered from newly formed co-operatives of village fishing communities, they had lain stinking in silos. The fishermen had not been compensated.

Most of the schemes, devised by self-seeking politicians, had come to grief. They passed the rusting hulk of a half-submerged tanker lying in the bay. There had never been the money or will to raise it, so it lay on its mudbank, the sea around it rainbowed with a slick of oil that still seeped from its drowned hull.

Max began to shiver. He looked out of the window into the brown depths of the palm plantations, where women stood twisting ropes of coir in the shade. Red castles of earth built by termites stood like milestones beside the road. The journey with the elephants, the facile display of emotion he had shown at the airport, the reality of the misery of the mother elephant at the loss of her baby and the horror on the airport road began to blur in Max's mind as drowsiness overcame him. His body shuddered with cold though the sun was still in the sky. He stifled a laugh as a faint feeling of hysteria rose within him. He thought of Alexander and of his 'baby' on its way to London Zoo. An immature giant delivered to penitential extinction. He checked himself as he saw Thomas eyeing him in the rear-view mirror. Max's thoughts lurched incoherently. Images of the burning bus, of the butchery and fear, the passion and despair of the mother elephant as majestically, impotently, she raged alone in her madness, remained branded on his mind.

It was hot and steamy, but he still felt unaccountably chilled. He wound up the window and then asked Thomas to wind up his. He shivered again. He was sweating and tingling with cold simultaneously. Clouds pressed lower against the waves, they in turn rolled higher and higher until they drowned the horizon. It was getting dark. A low sun squeezed out some of its colour between clouds. Palm trees thinned as the road turned towards the sea. Along the shore lines of fishermen were chanting for their catch as they hauled in their nets. Near-naked brown bodies gleamed as they struggled in the surf of large pre-monsoon waves. Mist was rising as the air cooled and touched hot dusty earth. They reached the headland at the curve of the bay. Village fires were already being lit. Trails of smoke rose from the depths of the palms. In the distance, suspended between the grey clouds and the silver ocean, sharper and darker and more extraordinary than anything else in the landscape, stood Max's own scrap of island. Max stopped the car on the road above the beach opposite the island. He got out. Thomas emerged from the passenger seat.

'Don't worry about the boat. Tide's out, I'll wade over,' said Max. Thomas protested but not too much for he was still feeling shaky.

'Look after yourself.' Max patted Thomas's shoulder and they parted company.

Monsoon clouds swelled on the horizon. Their leaden bulk darkened the ocean. Max shivered as a chill wind whispered past, raising hairs on his flesh. The bland humid air clung wet to his skin, and beads of sweat rolled down his forehead and rested on his eyebrows. The vein in his left temple, dilated, throbbed in time with his heart. A residue of alcohol burned in his stomach. Thunder rolled about aimlessly amongst cumulus clouds and the air was thick with the stink of brimstone.

The tide was on the turn, and the narrow shallow strait filling fast, swirling round the boundary rocks of Max's island, off an island, off a continent. He left the road and climbed down on to the beach. Looked out at the familiar hump of granite rising out of the sea, its outline like that of an elephant tethered offshore, trunk swinging gently in the waves. The throbbing in his head increased and his vision blurred. He closed his eyes and heard seabirds cry an anguished warning of the coming storm. Waves roared on the hidden seaward side. He walked down the beach, his shoes filling with soft sand, glanced back over his shoulder and watched the dim red glow of the tail-lamps of his car, as Thomas drove it away. It vanished along a mud track to where it would stand the night under a shelter of palm. Max removed his shoes and emptied them of sand.

The sky grew even darker, streaked with sulphur yellow. The sea was angry and seething where two currents met. The south-west monsoon, so predictable in its coming and so long in its torpid warning, arrived suddenly. Waves sucked and drew at rocks, swirled in dark caverns, evacuated and returned with a slap, refilling their gaping mouths. Under the bubbling sea spiny blue lobsters scrabbled to manoeuvre themselves backwards, to lurk in safety deep inside crevices, while limpets clamped on to their smooth anchorages. Small fish hid under overhangs and sea anemones withdrew their tentacles from damage and sealed their gelatinous mouths.

Max walked on down the beach, crossed wet sand and started to wade through shallow water towards his island; on top of which, entirely hidden by vegetation and invisible from the land, was an extraordinary folly of stone. Casuarina and temple trees stood taut against the sky, slanted by the winds that grazed away their symmetry. Behind their screen stood the house, blackened and stained with sooty moulds that festered in the tropical heat. Its walls were pierced by closed and shuttered windows. Its domed roof was hidden by a pediment supported by Ionic columns. Above and set behind was a crumbling balustrade, interrupted by sculptures of rampant beasts so desiccated by the sun and worn by the wind that their identities could only be guessed at. A semi-circular rotunda was attached to the west side, its floors carved from granite baserock, its walls broken by a succession of arches open to the elements. Beyond, on the southern seaward side, was a rough stone tower of more primitive design that plunged down sheer into the rock. Lush creepers and shrubs grew wild from every ledge and crevice, and swept down its walls, where they swung backwards and forwards in the monsoon winds.

Beyond the island lay three outcrops of perilous rocks each covered by scrub. In the past pirate fishermen had set lanterns on these rocks to lure unsuspecting ships to their doom. When the surf streamed in at night, and the plankton carried in its spume shimmered in the moonlight, they glittered and glowed. Waves flowed between small caverns beneath, causing a strange compelling music to drift across the sea.

The current was stronger than Max had anticipated and the water deep. Each high tide dragged new channels through the bed of sand. He lost his footing and his weak limbs flailed about. A large wave overwhelmed him and in panic he scrabbled at the slippery grey rock surfaces below a concrete landing stage. Moored alongside was a flat-bottomed boat that was used as a ferry to the main island when the tide was high. It wrenched at its mooring as it slapped its hull down on the surface of the incoming tide. He tried to rise, but lost his footing and slithered back. Skinned palms and a cut on his cheek spread with blood as it diluted with salt water. Max felt as if he were being excluded from gaining sanctuary. Thrust back by a force that denied him re-admission to his domain. He looked up from where he clawed at the rocks. The island stood dark and ruthless in the stormy light; Max, a soft-bodied creature with all his nerves flayed open and exposed, eased himself on to the rocks.

Some children playing between the twin hulls of a beached catamaran stopped and peered out across the strait at the man who lived on the island. Max waved to them. They returned to the intricacies of their game, their voices drowned by the increasingly turbulent sea.

He started to climb the one hundred and one stone steps towards his sanctuary. The rains approached from the south-west, preceded by an eerie stillness. Humidity rose to saturation. He felt he was suffocating; as if some awesome hand had moved in the heavens and placed a bell jar over him, capturing him in the torpid atmosphere in which he stood. His chest heaved. His lungs struggled to breathe in the last oxygen at the bottom of the jar. There was a rumble of thunder. The Portuguese used to call it the 'Elephanta'. A great herd had gathered to rage in the heavens. One or two huge raindrops, the size of pebbles, fell into the water, followed by a deluge which struck with such ferocity it fractured the surface of the sea and shot a pressed layer of brine into the air that stung both into a confusion of elements. Dripping, Max looked back at the shore through the drifting veils of rain. It was no more than a thin blue smudged line. He turned again to look up at his sanctuary, its outline almost indistinguishable from the dark cloud formation swelling behind.

A shaft of brilliant sunlight cut through a corridor of cloud like a ruler dividing day from night. It coloured the surface of the sea with iridescent nacre. Pierced between the shiny dark leaves of palms, casuarina and temple trees. Splattered its sulphurous light on stone walls. Turned glass into amber. Made umbrous purple shadows. Transformed the edifice that stood on top of the rock into a glittering gemstone, so extraordinary that it could have been conjured in a dream.

Awakened by lambent light, ghostly figures moved silkenly between rooms, leant out over balustrades, murmured secrets to one another on shady terraces, whispered beckoning sonnets to the winds. A slight breeze faltered off the sea. The narcotic musky scent of datura coiled about the lower rocks, intertwined with the heady breath of flowers of jasmine and caper bush. It swept up through branches of temple and ylang-ylang trees into arcaded passages before being lost as it floated out to sea. Insects danced on nectar. Birds of paradise vied their plumage. Duller coloured birds hid and sang with such melodic clarity, and complete oblivion of the approaching storm, that all Max's senses heightened in unison and he marvelled at the vision of his paradise.

At the top of the steps he stopped, legs aching and chest heaving with effort. Now again he felt fear, just a tremor, a flutter of fear. Fear that if not controlled could become rapacious. He checked himself and tried to calm his body's sensations of foreboding. He was home. He climbed on up the red-raked river of mud to a terrace and drew breath.

A pair of stone dolphins stood on either side of a flight of steps, each with eyes of lapis lazuli. They glinted in the last light of the sky. Tiny, bursting with raindrops, like those of the mother elephant he had left at the airport mourning the loss of her baby. Max was weak with the onset of fever, saturated with sweat, salt and rain. His heart continued to pump inside his body in a way that felt gross. Falteringly he bent down and searched for the key to the doors where it rested beneath a harp shell. The rain dripped from his hair and joined the sweat on his brow and rolled into his eyes. His face streamed with water and silently he began to cry. Tears and rain swept down his cheeks. A roar of thunder came out of the air. It exploded in a fiery crack that banished birds to their roosts. Max's heart leapt and stopped. He felt his pulse trying to regain its rhythm. He shuddered with cold as he turned the iron key in its lock.

On entering the circular Hall of the Lotus, so called

because its domed ceiling was painted with the flower, he found a kerosene lamp had been lit in anticipation of his return. Comforted by the contained warmth of the room and the shadowy yellow light, he closed the doors behind him; here, like the eater of the lotus, he longed to lose all memory.

Jaquitta, his Amazon green parrot, squawked a greeting from her cage in the centre of the room. He went to her and muttered soothingly. She arched her neck and lifted the feathers on the back of her head so that he might scratch her. Max obliged. He moved away and she clucked at him, craving more, watching him closely with her white feather-circled eyes. Unable to recapture his attention, she lifted one of her scaly padded feet and stroked herself, clucking and burbling a private language of comfort all her own.

Max stood in the hall removing his clothes. The buttons of his wet shirt seemed to have stuck fast in their holes and out of frustration he ripped at them. They snapped off, hit the floor and rolled away into inaccessible corners. He went to a side table and took a bottle of beer from an icebox. As he prised the metal top off it rolled away to join the buttons. His hands trembling, he poured carelessly. Beer foamed up over the rim and streamed down the outside of the glass. As he picked it up, it slipped from his weakened grasp and smashed. He stepped back with the shock and cut the ball of his foot. Shaking, Max limped upstairs to a bathroom and attended to his wound, scatterering lint and bandages everywhere in his feeble attempt to dress the cut. He pulled a bathrobe from where it had been carefully folded by Maria and wrapped his sore body inside it.

His mouth and throat were still dry and bitter with salt water. He limped to his bedroom, took out a bottle of whisky he kept there and returned to the bathroom. He picked up a stainless-steel toothmug, filled it half full of whisky and drowned it under the tap. He gulped and felt its tepid warmth trickle down into his empty stomach. His head was throbbing. The pain behind his eyes still pulsed in rhythm with his heartbeat. He refilled the mug with alcohol, feeling that if only he could blast at his bodily sensations fast and hard enough he would win the race that they were running despite him. He screwed up his eyes for a second. Lights coloured green and indigo blazed in an electric storm, like the photographers' flashbulbs that had surrounded him at the airport. He blinked to eradicate them, but even with his eyes wide open his vision was still smudged. Reflected in the looking glass in front of him he saw a haggard face, pale and drained. The gash on his cheek had swollen and a crust of madder-coloured blood had dried within its edge of proud flesh. He pushed back his limp hair from his temples and accidentally brushed the cut. A narrow trickle oozed down the side of his face and dripped on to the white porcelain of the basin. He dabbed at it with the sleeve of his robe.

Max limped back to his bedroom and got into bed.

He pulled up the starched linen sheet and waited for the whisky to take effect. Listened to the sounds of the rain above his head and the growing roar of the ocean below. Felt stinging pain from his wounds. The misery of the last weeks of his journey with the elephants to the airport would not leave him in peace. Alcohol and the onset of fever heightened the memory. He dared not close his eyes, so lay like a deranged man, limbs twitching involuntarily from time to time in response to their stabbing pain. Without knowing, he slept.

The herds of the Elephanta spilt out across the skies in their last rampage before dawn. Max woke. He lay in the dark, in a pool of sweat that had saturated his bedding. His limbs ached. His head ached. The walls of the shuttered room felt as if they had closed in about his bed. The bell jar had not been lifted and the air was still damp and thick.

Downstairs in the protracted half-light Jaquitta began to stir with the first calls of the morning. She clucked to herself, sleepily opening and closing her glazed eyes. With an almost imperceptible whistle she exhaled and tucked her head back into the puffed feathers of her neck. Melancholy suffused the early morning. Melancholy emanated from Max. Nothing escaped from it. Jaquitta, usually so cheerful, remained silent. Not another burble or whistle did she expel, but sat with her wing feathers hunched as if imitating a vulture. Outside the wind sighed through the trees and whispered over the waves and made a complex and fine music so taut that if it were to stretch its refrain any further it would turn into a lament. From somewhere came the faint scent of eucalyptus; it reminded Max of the hill country. Of the fires on the night stops, the elephants. His heart and stomach fluttered together in sickly despair.

Three

It was half-past six in the morning. The sun had hardly risen over the bank of cloud on the horizon. Maria and Thomas arrived in their boat laden with baskets of papaya, mangoes, breadfruit and all manner of fresh produce. They unloaded it on to the jetty and Thomas carried the provisions up the steps to the kitchen.

Beneath the house, hewn out of rock, and almost entirely covered in creepers, were several caverns. A row of troglodyte dwellings that at one time had been inhabited by monks, these served as the kitchen, a store-house for refrigerators and wood for cooking fires and warmth during the rainy season, a place for garden tools and a room in which Thomas and Maria rested during hot afternoons.

Only the kitchen had any external features, a window that opened on to the windward side of the island and an enormous pyramid of rough-hewn stones made to form a chimney that jutted from the top. Next to this was the largest cavern of all, a dining room with walls and floor of solid rock and an open shaft for ventilation in its roof. It was furnished with a large wooden table surrounded by elaborately carved Dutch ebony chairs, over which hung an enormous crystal candelabra. The walls were covered with brightly painted frescoes depicting lyrical scenes of the island. Exotic birds perched in dark green trees. Minstrels played their instruments to princes in their shade. Exquisite maidens with garlands of flowers danced in open glades. Wild beasts were tamed by the sound of a flute played on the shores of a moonlit lake. All backed by jungle and hills on which elephant and sambur grazed, while peacocks displayed their thousand eyes.

Thomas made a fire in the kitchen, to which he added some dry eucalyptus leaves, and scented wood-smoke funnelled up into the damp air. This morning there was silence between the couple. Maria suspected that Thomas had been drinking. On these occasions she would sometimes not speak to him for several days, but sit murmuring over her rosary with tearful eyes cast up towards a coloured portrait of the Blessed Virgin, praying for his soul. Thomas, recalcitrant, would finally succumb to her reproach and mutter his penance, secretly feeling wronged.

The night before, after dropping Max, Thomas had visited the palm-toddy stall. He needed a salve to relieve his memory of events on the airport road before he could face returning home. He recounted his story to the other men assembled there, standing under the dripping palm trees, sheltering from the storm. It was half-past nine when he finally parked the Pontiac behind the two-room brick house in which they lived. It was absolutely dark; he stumbled across a chair in the kitchen, knocking it over with a clatter. The noise of the tempest outside was great and Thomas was relieved that there was no sound from Maria. He lit a candle and sat down in the gloom to eat the cold curry and rice that she had left for him, wrapped in a banana leaf, on the table. A faded framed copy of *The Light of the World* was illuminated on the wall opposite him. Of all pictures with a pious theme he liked this one. The man looked friendly and his lantern glowed with a comforting light.

When Thomas eventually reached their bed he realised that Maria was awake. She lay on her side, her back turned, her stiff form jutting from the mattress like an impenetrable wall. He stretched out his hand to her for comfort and rested it on her plump forearm. She shrugged him off like an irritating insect, twisted away and let out an exasperated sigh of rejection. Thomas had lain awake in the stifling blackness of the tiny room, listening to the storm, fearful of Maria. When finally he slept he dreamed that he was still trapped in the airless boot of the Pontiac.

In the morning this tense silence still remained. Maria unfolded her starched white apron and tied it about her waist. She placed a cap on her head, pushing back her black curly hair with red plastic grips before she knelt upon the polished stone floor of the kitchen and said her first prayers. Thomas stepped outside, glad to be away from Maria. Whilst she prayed, he started about his duties.

Thomas and Maria lived ordered lives. The nuns had taught them that the devil was always looking for an opportunity to enter a house and he would seize on chaos, for the devil thrived on mayhem. Thomas had seen evidence of this in the garden. If paths and terraces were not swept and dead material removed every day, insects and grubs gathered and disease spread to the plants. Just as vermin would enter the kitchen, if it were not scrubbed and swept daily. Constant fear of the devil and their faith in God and the Holy Mother consumed their lives, but it had not preserved their only son from premature death. When Father Miguel had brushed them aside to deliver extreme unction, and the boy had coughed out his last breath as the censer swung to and fro over his tiny limp body, Thomas had doubted his faith. Maria was unaware of his scepticism, for he clung on to religious ritual like a magic charm, unable entirely to disentangle himself from the fallacies of sin. He had seen the worst visited upon the best and holiest of men and women. He had not believed Father Miguel when he told them that they were blessed to have been chosen for this sacrifice. As he climbed up the steps to the main house Thomas heard Maria saying her rosary in the kitchen below.

Max lay in his bed in his room. He heard Thomas leave the kitchen by the garden path and begin to mount the steps. Thomas paused at the top, where he found a clear plastic bag containing Max's shoes, his wallet and watch. He bent down to pick it up, disturbed to find these valuables left out for the night. Small pools of water that had gathered in the folds from the rains of the previous night trickled between his fingers to the ground. Unfastening the bag, he took out the watch. Its glass was shattered and it had stopped at six o'clock. He shook it and held it to his ear, but there was no sound from the movement. He opened the door of the hall and entered; he placed Max's watch beside his wallet on a low mahogany table just inside the door and continued with his morning ritual. Raising and lowering blinds, adjusting, opening and closing windows and shutters to create the maximum shade and flow of air through the interior.

Jaquitta roused herself from her torpor and became excited at the prospect of a fresh supply of fruit and seeds. She bobbed up and down on her perch, burbling and whistling for Thomas's attention. He opened the door of her cage and she retreated to the furthest bars, where she clung upside down twisting and craning her head, watching his every move. As soon as he had finished, she raced down to the fresh seed and went at it with such frenzy that she scattered half the contents of the container on to the silver sand at the bottom of her cage. Thomas was captivated by the bird's antics and the welcome she always gave to him. She pressed herself tight against the bars close to where he stood and burbled out her repertoire of repetitive phrases and half-learnt nursery rhymes. Her recital culminated in a shriek of excitable laughter.

On the far side of the room Thomas noticed Max's shirt and other garments lying on the floor. He left the bird and crossed the room to pick them up. The damp clothes had left pale patches on the polished teak. Thomas bent down and rubbed at them hard with a cloth from his pocket but they didn't come out. Maria would discover the mess and add it to his other misdemeanours. Resigned, he went back to the kitchen with the clothes and placed them in a basket to be dealt with by the cleaning girl, Pyhia, when she arrived.

He went outside to the gardens to pick fresh flowers. When he had gathered what he required he carried them down to the garden room and arranged them in vases before returning each to its allotted position in the house. Thomas may have been a simple man, but he had innate artistry. He could set a creamy waxed bloom to float in the centre of a pool of water and it would be perfect. He would invent surprises by mixing the unexpected, but whatever he did with scent or petal or colour it had an equilibrium, a harmony that enchanted every morning. His secret dream was that one day he would leave the small settlement in which they lived and go to the city, where he would have a flower and garland stall. Perhaps in one of the tourist hotels. Maybe eventually his own shop.

Max lay tangled in his sweaty sheets. His temperature

had almost returned to normal. A dust-filled sunbeam lit the bleached hairs on his forearm. Along its length, through half-closed eyes, he saw cities and landscapes and towards his elbow, a herd of grazing elephant. He flung his arm away from the light and screwed up his eyes to eradicate the image. Mixed with the scent of eucalyptus came the smell of coffee. The mere thought of his breakfast being prepared caused the acid to rise in his empty stomach. He imagined Maria scooping out the stringy flesh of fresh mangoes and squeezing it with her fingers, the thick liquid clinging to the sides of the glass. The orange-coloured segment of papaya already coated his mouth as its glossy black pips were teased away from its flesh, scooped out and thrown away into a bin. The acidity of the limes she sliced, the pungent smell of fresh brewed coffee repulsed him.

Thomas's footsteps moved nearer his bedroom. The coming confrontation with the man opening the door was too much for Max. He twisted in his bed and pulled a corner of his sheet over his eyes to protect them from the inevitable blast of light. Thomas went into the bathroom. He set down a vase of tuberose on the table under the window and began to draw water. As he stood over the gushing taps he noticed some streaks of what looked like dried blood on the rim of the bath. He turned, and saw bloodstained bandages and cotton wool scattered about the floor. Felt a tremor of fright. He had already suspected that something was wrong – the watch, the ripped shirt on the floor downstairs – but he had been more preoccupied with Maria's accusatory sullenness. Hesitantly he knocked at the door of Max's bedroom. Without waiting for a reply he entered the dimly lit room, passed through the sunbeam and yanked at the cords of the blinds. With a loud snap they rolled upwards towards the ceiling. Through the tight weave of his sheets Max screwed up his eyes against the blinding force of the light. He had read once that it was possible to traumatise a perfectly normal child into an introverted, incommunicable infant just by shocking its senses violently. He turned in his bed and pressed his face down into his damp pillow, suffocating himself.

Thomas crossed the room, put his hand gingerly on Max's shoulder and said in a concerned voice, 'Sir, are you unwell? This is not good. Sir, sir?'

Max exhaled, a choked sigh that was lost in the heat of his own breath. He raised himself on one elbow for a moment like a wounded animal then slumped and turned away, the man's words ebbing and flowing in his ears. Thomas's attentive presence irritated him. He wanted nothing more than to be left alone. He could hear Maria carrying up the breakfast tray and setting it down on a table outside on the terrace. Max felt mounting claustrophobia. Thomas nervously retreated back to the bath and turned off the taps.

Max got up and dragged himself towards his bathroom. He sank his aching limbs under the warm water in the tub. He submerged his head, in an attempt to make all of his body reach the same temperature. There was an ache in his groin, in his side and under his armpits. The pain in his cut foot persisted. He held his breath and rested under the surface. In the silence he felt the pump of his heart. With effort he remained underwater, listening to the sounds in his ears of each auricle and ventricle opening and closing. He felt the movement of his diaphragm expanding his lungs and letting them collapse with a wheeze of exhaled air. Fingers and toes were reduced to sharp pointed pains that ran along paths away from him. Vessels at the back of his eyes, on the outside of his cranium, seemed filled to bursting and echoed with the sharp stabbing pulse of his life. Bright patterns of light jagged before his eyes as if they were the flickering screens of a life-support machine. Then from somewhere unidentified, from the silent box of his brain, came a noise, dull and continuous. He listened, utterly absorbed by it as the pitch rose higher and higher as if someone outside were controlling the knob on this apparatus. Swallowed up by noise he listened as it changed from its former intensity and seemingly thinned to the width of a human hair, stretched out into a scream so intolerable in its pitch that all he could record was pain. His submerged body did not react until his lungs seemed about to burst. He shuddered in a spasm and jerked out of the water. Slumped on the floor he recognised that what he heard was the call and then the cry of the mother elephant, a sound like hot wires sawing through his skull.

From his bedroom, a rattle as Maria replaced ice in its

container. Then the sharp crack of linen as she shook out the sheets and lowered them on to his bed. He listened to her plumping his pillows before pulling down the blind. Max closed his eyes and saw only glaring light. Light so intense that he might have been standing on some sun-scorched shore. He blinked and white went blue, the blue of flax flowers from which sheets were made, blue of Pyhia's robes. He opened his eyes and the only light that entered the room through the slatted shutter jagged like the last reel of a film as it winds off the spool and celluloid clicks through the projector. Images flashed and, as they faded, his nightmare concentrated into black.

There was a knock on the door. Thomas entered carrying a pile of fresh towels and a robe. He came into the bathroom, dropped his load and hurriedly went to help Max get up from where he was lying in a pool of water beside the bath. He sat him down on a stool and draped the bathrobe over Max's shoulders.

'Sir, have you fever? Shall I fetch aspirin?'

'It's all right, Thomas, I . . .' He searched for an explanation. 'Slipped . . . leave me now, I'm all right, just leave me please, alone,' said Max in a confused and exasperated tone. 'OK . . . Yes, fetch aspirin.'

Thomas retreated, upset at his rejection. Put his ear to the door for a few moments until he heard the reassuring rush of water into the handbasin. Max looked at himself through the flashes of colour still hurling themselves about in front of his eyes. He splashed his face with cold water and reached for his shaving brush, but his trembling hand knocked it off the shelf and it rolled down on to the floor. 'Blast it,' he groaned. He picked up a towel and hurriedly dried the water from the bristles on his chin and staggered back to bed.

Thomas removed the uneaten breakfast and returned to the kitchen, where Maria was standing over a boiling mixture of rice and lentils in broth. She had concluded, having mopped up spilt beer and disposed of broken glass and an empty whisky bottle, that Max, like her husband, was suffering from a hangover.

'Thomas, did you hear me?' she called out in a shrill voice, not realising that he was standing behind her. She stirred the gluey bubbling mixture in the pan as if it were a religious duty. 'You're no better than one another. I despair for both of you.'

Thomas was not so sure that Max had a hangover. Even though he had smelt the drink on his breath and seen how unsteady he had been as he walked across the car park at the airport the previous afternoon, he assumed that his master was exhausted from the long journey with the elephants. He remembered how Max had sweated and shivered in the car. Malarial fever was sweeping through some of the villages at this season of the year. But he dismissed these thoughts from his mind and said nothing to Maria. It would have only angered her. She would think that he was trying to make excuses for his master and for himself. Dutifully he did as his wife prescribed and carried the rice and lentils upstairs.

Max was sitting up in bed, somewhat recovered. He

accepted the rice and began to eat. Thomas, reassured, wondered whether perhaps Maria had been correct in her diagnosis. They had both suffered the day before. He felt a degree of comradeship with his master. Thomas placed the aspirin tablets and a fresh flask of chilled water on the table beside Max's bed and hovered about the room dusting around ornaments and adjusting flowers, occasionally glancing at Max.

Max began to be irrationally irritated by the man's fluttering attentions. Again he wanted nothing more than to be left alone.

'You're going to the orphanage this weekend?' On the last weekend of every month Thomas and Maria went to visit an orphanage on the outskirts of the city. Apart from Sunday afternoons this was the only time they took off.

'Yes, sir, if you are well enough. Maria has everything in order and Pyhia will come over to attend to you.' Thomas knew that this would please Max, and indeed he looked up and tried a smile.

'Is there anything I can do for you before we go?'

Max shook his head. 'Go, Thomas. That journey . . .' His voice tailed off and he lay back on the soft down pillows and closed his eyes as if to sleep. Thomas left, relieved that Max seemed better. That weekend was an important visit to the orphanage, for Father Miguel had promised them a little boy for adoption. This was to be their first meeting.

*   *   *

Settled, Max conjured up a vision of Pyhia's beautiful face. He supposed that Maria knew how he felt about Pyhia. She had behaved like a harridan to the girl ever since she had been engaged to clean the house and do the washing after her work at the coir factory. Pyhia was a Buddhist, a non-believer as far as Maria was concerned, and her soul was in mortal danger. Daily she drove the frail girl on and on, to sweep and scour and scrub the floors until they shone. It was as if she expected her to do eternal penance for the original sin that possessed her. While Maria cooked, and from her kitchen came delights set out on rosewood- and mahogany-inlaid trays covered with starched linen, Pyhia laboured with heavy buckets, scrubbed the terraces, scoured the burnt and blackened pots and was seldom allowed to be seen, particularly by Max. Maria had forbidden her to enter his quarters and it had become Thomas's task to attend to those rooms. Maria considered the younger woman to be beneath her. They had a house built of brick. A painted plaster statue of the Virgin and a framed picture of Christ crowned in thorns revealing his sacred red bleeding heart from beneath his robes. A wooden crucifix hung above their bed and a metal one about Maria's neck.

Max waited, listened for silence, then got out of bed and went to the window. He lifted the blind a fraction so as not to be observed. Below on the jetty Thomas and Maria were getting into their boat. Max felt free and alone, as they cast off and headed for the opposite shore. He waited for some moments, listened in the gloom for

71

any sounds of life. When confident that they would not return, he went down to the Hall of the Lotus. He paced about the room like a child discovering unexpectedly that all the adults have gone away and he has been left alone. The familiar became intimidating. The room seemed larger than he remembered, its shadows darker and more secret. Furniture loomed at him. Portraits seemingly came to life, their eyes followed his every move. Things he had put down thoughtlessly had already become dusty and lifeless.

Jaquitta scrabbled about her cage, walking from perch to perch via the bars. At each level, she cocked her head on one side and peered out inquisitively at Max from another angle. He went to her and together they cooed comfort to one another. He put his finger through the bars and scratched the back of her neck.

For the remainder of the morning he moved distractedly about the empty rooms. He felt utterly and painfully alone. Overwhelmed by a sense of impending doom. There was no longer any solace in the perfection that he had created for himself. This paradise, this shell, so carefully constructed, inviolable and permanent, had suddenly lost its solidity. As if it would only take a slight wind to lift it all aloft, spin it and turn it upside down and inside out on its airy current. All that had once been his consolation seemed only to point up the fragility of his hedonistic existence. Every time that Max had been alone in his sanctuary before it had enchanted him with its tranquillity and beauty and absolute peace.

But the constancy, the blissful isolation of living on an island, a small star at the edge of a galaxy, removed from the turmoil and excess of the outside world, had unaccountably fled. Outside the sun shone but in the distance was the threat of further thunder.

He turned his back on the room and crossed the stone slab of a bridge that separated the main building from the tower. He climbed the spiral staircase to the top, then sat down at his desk in the centre of the turret room and looked out blankly towards the ocean. The tower was crammed with paper. Personal letters, bills, photographs, private journals, fragments of his life. About the walls were shelves that were designed in a spiral so that walking along them was like entering the cavernous shell of a snail, lined with paper. The damp and humid air, combined with water vapour off the sea, had fused this burden of paper together. Yellowed and musty, their ink smudged and indecipherable, the pages had become inseparable. The mass of material had turned into a giant papier mâché sculpture, filling the room. It was Max's entire correspondence with the world outside and it was now unreadable. He inhabited a past that could never be reviewed by prying curiosity.

Pyhia arrived; the wind brought the sounds of her down below in the kitchen. He listened and imagined her as her bare feet slapped lightly over the flagstones, unaware of his presence. There was the occasional clatter as she set down a bucket of water and the swish of a mop as she swabbed the floors. For half an hour, an hour, he sat in melancholy longing for her to climb the stair and find him. The sound of her moving about fuelled his new-found loneliness.

Once he had visited the coir factory where he had been told that she worked. Many Europeans had taken islanders as mistresses or honorary wives. They rarely actually married the women. From the day that he had first engaged Pyhia to work for him Max had harboured a fantasy that she would be appropriate for that role. He knew she was unmarried. The visit to the coir factory had been the only positive move he had made to discover more of her life, except in his imagination. So Pyhia had remained just out of reach but always present in his daily life. That day he had watched the women, some little more than children, as they sat under palm roofs in dark sheds; cutting and dressing coconut fibre, dyeing it in vats, knotting it on to looms. The bulbous factory manager showed him around. He accustomed his eyes to the terrible dusty gloom. Watched thin workers shaving surfaces off mats. Women bent over their work in that dreary limbo, and always outside was the light. For a factory it was strangely silent. Only the odd cough from the workers or the thunder of a grey langur or a mongoose across the corrugated-iron roof.

He pretended that he was not looking for Pyhia, but his eyes furtively scanned the arms of the faceless workers as they sat, heads bowed, knotting and combing. Some had skins of lizard, some skins of silk, but he was looking for a forearm dusted with the softest fur. He did not find her and was strangely relieved that he had been misinformed and that she was not condemned to this place. But, as he passed along the rows of women he heard stifled giggles and saw knowing looks exchanged between them. It might have been his imagination, but he thought that they all knew for whom he was searching. Suddenly he felt utterly disgusting, like a man in a brothel making his selection. Gratefully he returned to the manager's office, where he was offered refreshment.

Unnoticed, Pyhia had entered the room carrying a tin tray on which rested two cups of milky brown tea and a bowl of sugar. When she placed the tray on the table between them, he saw the forearm that he had been seeking and looked up. She smiled at the two men. He ached to reach out and touch her but, as if she had sensed his desire, she lifted both her arms and modestly covered her face with her robe before retreating towards the door. She vanished like a wraith. He sat opposite the fat, contented manager and wondered why it was Pyhia who had brought their tea. As he studied the man he realised that these special duties probably extended further than the serving of refreshment. Sick with disgust and jealousy, he made a feeble excuse about a forgotten appointment and left his tea untouched on the tray.

Although the memory of that morning and what he thought had been Pyhia's reaction to him made him squirm, he could no longer endure his solitude. Finally he got up and went downstairs to find her.

Just as he opened the door of the Hall of the Lotus

he heard a startled cry. Across the room, framed in the opposite doorway, stood Pyhia. Unaccountably the sight of the beautiful young girl took him by surprise. She stood there in silence looking directly at his stiffened shamble of limbs. Then she withdrew into the light, slowly closing the door into its frame until it was shut. The blade of the lock jagged back with a small click, the handle revolved half a turn. That click, heard across the expanse of teak floorboards, left Max bereft in the empty room. With her retreat from his presence he realised that he was no better to her than the fat old factory manager who blackmailed the youngest and prettiest girls into giving him sexual favours; threatening them with the fear of losing their livelihoods.

Max stood still, too sick with himself to call out after her. He listened as Pyhia ran away from him, down the path to the sea. She untied the boat from its mooring beside the landing stage, jumped in and took up the oars and rowed herself away from the island back towards the beach.

Max went to the window and watched her slip away from him. A narrow rime of foam at the bows of the boat parted on either side of its hull. The two lines of wash angled away from one another, separated and were lost on their divergent course through the sea.

In that instant something slight and almost indefinable happened. Until then his life had held together cohesively in a rounded body, like a bubble of mercury rolling about in the cupped palm of his hand. He clenched

76

his fist as if to grasp what had once seemed unified and complete. Beads of quicksilver shot out between his fingers, exploded into a thousand atoms and slipped away. He stood at the window gazing after the girl. Left to endure the purgatory of his sickness alone.

He walked slowly around the entire house, closing all the windows, pulling down each blind in turn and carefully locking all the shutters before retreating upstairs to his bed. He lay there concentrating on the dim bands of light that crisscrossed the interior of the room. A cry strangled in his throat as he lay immobile, sweating with disease behind the barricaded walls of his mausoleum.

Pyhia would not leave his thoughts that night. If he closed his eyes, her elfin face and the fixed stare of her large brown eyes were in front of him. If he dreamed, it was of her: dancing, tiny golden feet in the sand. A thin blue flax flower swaying in the simmering heat of the midday air; bleached against the fierce aquamarine of the water and the pink coral sand. He hardly dared to blink in case his vision might be destroyed, so he held his eyelids fast to take in that second of exquisite memory. Pyhia, the sunlight, and the dappled shade of the coconut palms. She slid down to rest at the foot of one of the trees, her head uncovered, the length of her robe looped about her hips and bound her breast, but her midriff was bare, exposing her thin frame. The memory aroused him and he despised himself for the lust he felt. Pyhia got up, unwrapped the faded blue fabric from her body and cast it into the shade; ran naked across the sand into the surf. She emerged, her skin glistening, slowly arched her arms above her head and took a comb out of her hair; it uncurled and fell loose down her bronze back. Max noticed the down on her forearms and imagined that she stretched out towards him in a welcoming embrace. He smelt the sandalwood scent of her skin and felt her long thick hair against his breast.

His body juddered him awake and he lay conscious, painfully conscious. Once he called out her name, but the sound of his voice made an empty noise in the room. He turned his aching limbs and reached out across the sheets to where he imagined she lay beside him. He roused himself and knelt over her beautiful spectral form. In his hands were white flowers of jasmine which he laced intricately amongst her dark pubic hairs. As his hands and eyes worked down over the soft furred mound and between her parted thighs, he was tempted to place his fingers inside the damp pink crevice between her legs. But he could not and, shamefaced, plucked more flowers from the air and placed them in the hollows under her arms. Through the blueish-black hair on her brow he wove a garland and finally he laid a creamy camellia between her breasts. As if drugged by scent and sleep, she did not move but lay like Titania, inviolable in her secret bower.

Max turned away. Sick with himself as he felt a pulse quicken in his groin. He rolled over on his bed and pressed himself hard face down, sweating, breathing heavily, his heart racing. He turned over on to his back and lay on the sticky patch of semen on his sheets and felt the full grossness of his lust.

Delirious with fever and suffering delusions, his vision of Pyhia fled and in her place beside him lay Olivia, Alexander's wife, a hard and brittle figure. The moon had risen and was full and its light squeezed between the slats of the shutters and fell on her ashen naked body in zebra bands. She turned her head and whispered in his ear like the sirens and breathed a sweet and devilish music that filled the room. Max felt his disembodied frame being carried on a current that caught him up and swept him away, dragging him round the curve of the earth, ever south towards Antarctic seas. The water cooled, the sky was an intense blue and fragments of ice drifted about him. His entire body shuddered. An ache developed in his right side. His liver had swollen. On and on he floated, was locked into ice floes that ground and twisted and churned and chilled his flesh. He lay trapped in a desert of ice that was expanding against his ribs, squeezing each muscle, sinew, nerve and organ in turn until all feeling had gone. His heart went on pumping its solitary comfort into tissue seized in trauma until at last arms, legs, bowels, and tongue ceased to receive the flow. Just a core pulsed, heart to brain and brain to heart; back and forth, back and forth, through its last narrow channel between life and death. Immobile, he lay listening to its beat. He thought that his brain might scream but it was incapable of feeling pain. Snow fell and he took comfort from its swaddling embrace, felt transformed into some ancient fossil whose bulk, like that of such an extinct creature, was sinking slowly down through a millennium of silt, perfectly preserved under a crust of ice. His heart clotted.

Olivia spread herself across the bed. She took on the form of a bird. Her skin was softly feathered. From her open mouth a pointed tongue extended like a hungry squab. Her eyes were hard and black with a moon reflected in each so that they shone with a cold light. She was exquisite. Her thick dark hair coiled like serpents on the pillows. Max started from his dreams and felt sweat drip from all over his body and saturate the sheets. He blinked but the apparition of Olivia would not vanish. Her mouth opened and closed, sucking his body closer to hers. He averted his eyes and confusion enclosed his senses. The powerful scent of tuberose standing in a vase on the table beneath the window wove itself through the fibres of the linen sheets on the bed. Max was consumed by this succubus. He throbbed within the darkness of her body. Started to fight for his life. Covered with the smell of sex, he fled.

Outside there was silence. The house was still, but behind him in his bed he imagined Olivia waiting for him. Fermenting between the sheets, flagrant, white, naked, immovable. A she-devil dancing through his night. Max lit a cigarette but it tasted foul. After one deep breath he threw it away. He watched until the small red glow amongst the falling blooms of the Queen of the Night went out. He sat down and lit another. He coiled a towel around his waist and waited. There was no sound from his bedroom. She had not left. She was not sleeping. Her silence threatened him. He lit another cigarette and poured himself a drink. He waited for her siren call. Max plucked a pink hibiscus from where it grew and threw the flower down over the wall. Watched it drift his scentless desire to the terrace below. It could have been the wind or the rising waves that flowed like treacle about the rocks, but from the bedroom he was sure that he heard Olivia laugh. A bitter twisted laugh. As Max listened he recoiled. The succubus that had come to him was possessed by hate, tearing at every auricle and ventricle of his heart.

He did not return to his bed that night but sat up until dawn, plagued by his fever. When the light came and he finally re-entered his bedroom he thought that he still smelt the musk of Olivia's scent.

The monsoon rain was torrential. It pelted on roof-tiles and flooded over gutters and fell in sheets on to terraces, sweeping away the light soil and exposing the red granite underlay. The palms bent and swayed. The blossom was stripped from every tree and shrub and lay in sodden stained heaps upon the ground. Whipped up by the wind, the sea had doubled its depth and rose in huge tongues of waves that raced headlong towards the island from all sides, crashing their immense volume on to the rocks; spouts of spray rose into the air and were caught

81

and carried in haphazard salty clouds over the tops of the trees. All sight of land had vanished and if a man had been able to stand against the tyrannical gusting gale on the shore there would have been no sign of Max's island. It was lost in elemental chaos. Shrouded and alone like a tiny boat without a man at the helm; a piece of flotsam delivered up to the storm.

Downstairs, stranded in the centre of the Hall of the Lotus, Jaquitta squawked and sang, danced upon her perch and shrieked insanely. The shutters rattled at their fastenings and pools of water lay on the shiny wooden floors where they had been blown in through gaps under doors. Geckos called out as they feasted on sheltering insects.

Upstairs, demented by fever, Max twisted and turned in his bed. His temperature was dangerously high. He no longer felt pain in his limbs. He felt no physical pain at all. He dreamed a troubled dream, a disembodied dream of decay. As the interior of the house dripped, water stained the walls where it had been blown up under the tiles. Beams and rafters that should have supported roofs were gorged on by termites and lay rotting on marble floors. Staircases twisted nightmarishly up into the air, leading nowhere. Ferns sprouted in dank shadow, their fronds rapidly uncurling leaves of brilliant green in their anxiety to smother. Snakes and scorpions entered the house in search of a dry haven from the storm. They slithered and crawled up the mouldy walls, through drains, along gutters, out of the dark of plugholes.

The bedroom floor became a seething mass beneath him. Insects of every description entered his room. Under the doors and through crevices they squeezed their armour-plated bodies. They flew in through the windows. Drowned in the water jugs. Landed and clustered on any available surface. Copulated and multiplied until the entire room was a scrabbling mass of legs and wings and compound eyes and searching antennae. They made fast little animated runs of a few millimetres at a time towards his bed, crawled up its legs and swarmed over the counterpane. Ran over his flesh before they entered through the orifices of his body and scrabbled along veins and arteries, multiplying as they went and destroying the cells in his blood.

Outside the sea had boiled itself away and over the grey salty landscape a terrifying sun burned in the sky. On cracked dusty earth lay desiccated fish whose flesh was being stripped from their bones by scavenging seabirds. Banks, forested with pastel-coloured corals, jutted from the sand-sea. Clusters of bivalves gaped with open mouths and a terrible stench circled on the light breeze. Further out, silhouetted against the light, a shoal of porpoise lay beached, their jaws still curled up in a smile. On their backs stood dogs, snarling and snapping at one another as each tugged from the corpses its prize of meat. There was no one on the beach. The fishermen's canoes and catamarans lay broken; heaped one upon another, it was as if they had been seized in a whirlwind and dumped like driftwood after the storm. Many of the palm trees had been snapped like pencils and the flimsy village houses had been swept away. In the barren jungle there was no sign of life. The only sound to be heard was the yelps of pye-dogs. Ownerless, barking amongst the ruins of the temples of the Pharaohs, Delphi and in the underground passages of the Colosseum. From a small hill on the Palatine, Max saw them roaming in packs around the Forum. Their snuffles and barks echoed through the ruins of a civilisation. They urinated and defecated in the house of the Vestals. They gnawed on the corpses of the dead and unearthed the buried. Then, howling their lament, they too finally died in the dust of a civilisation.

Max got up from his sickbed. His tongue had swollen inside his mouth and his lips were shiny and cracked. There was grey stubble on his chin. His eyes, discoloured and traced with reddened veins, stared out of the cavities of their sockets. His skin was yellow and stretched taut against the bones of his face. The flesh on his emaciated body sagged over muscles that had no tone or strength. His hair had turned white. He was an old man. Falteringly he dressed himself in a luridly coloured kaftan that hung on a peg on the back of the door. It made him look faintly comical, like an old wizard who had escaped from the pages of a storybook.

He found his way downstairs, Jaquitta remained silent when he entered the room. Slowly she stretched each of her wings in turn, revealing her gaudy flight feathers, then ruffled herself and started to coo tenderly at Max.

Outside the monsoon had passed, leaving behind it the debris of the storm. He fumbled in his pocket for a cigarette. Lit it and choked, but he went on. He liked the foul taste of the tobacco in his mouth and the stinging warmth of the smoke as he inhaled it into his lungs and let it out through his nostrils. He went outside. The sun was bright and the air clear. The sea had subsided and tiny wavelets swirled in all directions catching the light. He walked falteringly down the path towards the southern side of his kingdom, sat down on a marble bench and contemplated the huge expanse of ocean that stretched out before him across the equator to the Antarctic.

There was no sign of anyone. Thomas had not returned. No smell from the kitchen. No plume of smoke from the stack. No sound of Maria at prayer. He looked up at the tattered brown leaves of the king palms as they waved about above his head in the breeze. A bird began to sing. Resounding on the inner membrane, the melody came like pain to his ears. Max raised his hands and clapped them together. The bird flew away. He continued to stare out to sea. A shoal of flying fish leapt and sparkled above the waves. As his weakened eyes gazed into the blinding white light, the fish were transformed. Mermaids, with naked torsos, flaxen hair and shining tails, cavorted through the sparkling water. The huge coloured scales on their fish-like tails shot rainbows up into the air. Their joyful, lithe, immature bodies were those of children. Hundreds of them. Perfect. Swimming towards his island. They leapt like porpoises, arched through the air. Splashed down below the surface. Rose up again through sheer exuberance. Max pulled hard on his cigarette and smiled. He felt a pulse of pleasure that had been lost to him since his return. He watched their bliss as they danced between the waves. A slight wind sheered across the surface of the sea. The air chilled. He did not feel it. The cigarette's glow died between his lips. He looked on. Their numbers strangely thinned. For each score that hit the water only a handful rose to leap again. Slowly Max realised that they were drowning. Dying in shoals as they sank beneath the waves. The sea was poisoned. The air they gasped was poisoned. They were making their last glorious leaps not with joy but in agony. The tails of some of the mermaids separated from their bodies. Twitching and writhing independently with a life and energy that could never have been possible if a brain and nervous system were functioning and in control. Still they swam towards him, reflex shamming life. Rising out of the water and splashing on to the rocks. Standing and spinning on the tips of their tails, they slithered towards his outstretched arms as he went rushing to embrace them.

One after another they tumbled and died. Their powerful tails slapped against the jagged wet rocks in frenzy with the remains of their lives. Max closed his eyelids and wept, but no tears came. His eyeballs burned, he sobbed and shuddered, but his tear ducts were dry.

When he opened his eyes a pale blue-skinned girl with a black skein of sodden hair was floundering in the yellow surf foaming at his feet. He stretched out his hand, she took it and he pulled her up on to the rocks. Slowly, together, the shining fish-like girl and the old man made their way up the steep rocky path towards the house together. The sun went behind a cloud and an icy wind got up. It roared through the trees and scorched their succulent tropical leaves. Around the island the surface of the sea froze and an unnatural rime of winter chilled the earth. On top of the house cranes gathered, waiting to suck the breath of the sick. Together they struggled against the gale down to Thomas's cavern. Max's legs so weak they would hardly carry him. The tail fin of the girl stuck to the icy path. Several times he bent down and used the slight warmth in his hands to free her from where she stood. Inside the cavern was dark. He sat her down on a rocky ledge and lifted her sodden windswept hair from her eyes. She stared up at him with a pleading, lifeless look. 'Wait,' he said, 'there is something I must do.' Outside icicles were forming from the roof of the cave. Growing so fast that an impenetrable curtain was forming between them and the rest of the world. Desperately Max searched the darkening room. The fish-girl sat slumped opposite him. He looked down at her and the terrifying truth came to him that these children had been so damaged that their human forms no longer existed; only these mutations, these sad chimera.

Propped up in the corner was a yellow parcel. Arrived on a packet boat from China. Inside a peony, a black tree peony. Celebrated by the Chinese as the king of the flowers. Adorning the elaborately ornate articles of the trousseaux of imperial princesses. Beloved by the emperors of the T'ang and Ming dynasties. The flower of the phoenix, resurrection and spring. John Gerard in his *Herball* wrote that its most effective use was for those afflicted by nightmare.

With new-found strength he lifted the wrapped package under one arm and with the other helped the fish-girl to stand. They shattered the icicles as they left the cavern and made their way back up the path to the highest point on the island. The tropical plants had all withered and died. The palms had petrified. Max chipped away at the frosty soil in an attempt to dig a hole. His fingers turned blue, to the colour of the fish-girl's skin. It began to snow, filling his hair and beard. The fish-girl stood rooted to the ground, watching with her sad black eyes, swaying slightly in the gale. He unravelled the packet. Straw and paper blew about. Tenderly he lowered the plant into the soil. Snow was mounting about them and starting to drift. Max stood back in triumph and brushed the snowflakes from his eyes. The plant stood firm against the gale. Slowly its leaves unfurled and the buds burst open to reveal black flowers. A scent of magical intensity was released into the cold air. But it did not smell of spring, of hope or a new beginning. It was the acrid stench of fire and brimstone and damnation. As he stared into the velvet blackness of the expanded petals and drew breath, his nostrils filled with the scent of the flowers of Hell.

* * *

Max sat in his room in the tower. Outside he could hear the storm raging and the sweet song of the sirens calling for him across the waves, promising foreknowledge of the future of the earth. Flashes of lightning rent the sky. Cinders from his overflowing ashtray drifted about as Max exhaled a forlorn sigh. Beside him on his desk stood a pewter statue of a mermaid; the metal glowed with a bluish bloom in the lamplight. Next to it was a bell jar filled with captive mosquitoes. In front of him a pistol. He shuddered. Felt an acute sensation of the pain of cold in a hot climate. He raised the tip of the barrel to his lips – they twitched as the metal touched their fine dry skin – and pressed it deep into his mouth. Max shot himself. He thought it the only sane thing to do.

The wind steadied and the rain stopped. The ocean was nothing more than a faint roar. The herds of the Elephanta left the skies. Kerosene lamps were lit in the village on the other side and plumes of wood-smoke trailed up through the palms. Across the water could be heard the chatter of villagers returning home from the fields, and the sound of pye-dogs baying at the moon.

Four

Terrorists had taken over the game reserve. With the connivance of men like Siri they had exterminated the last herd of elephants. The animals had been easy pickings whilst gathered in great numbers at the remaining waterholes.

When Alexander and his crew arrived at the gates of the sanctuary with sheaves of official passes and permits to film they had expected some form of reception. Everybody knew Alexander's name and face, he had appeared on Mannar Island television with the President to thank the people for their gift of the baby male elephant to London Zoo. They had seen the film of Max at the airport. Before leaving the capital the Minister for the Environment had assured them that his most senior trackers and guides had been contacted and would be assembled in readiness. Vehicles would be supplied and every assistance given during filming. Those endless days of appointments with bureaucrats, hours spent filling out forms in triplicate in dismal stuffy offices with beguilingly competent officials, took on an air of wasted frustration. After all those smiling promises and reassurances, they were now alone in this godforsaken scrub with no maps of tracks or information on the position of waterholes and no knowledge of the terrain. No idea where the nearest tank was, even less where to find those rare herds of elephant.

Alexander saw that his crew was getting edgy. The intolerable heat of the monsoon season, the intermittent storms and the forsaken look of the game reserve offices seemed to offer little prospect of filming that day. He got down from their Land Rover and entered a green-painted wooden building just inside the gates. The floor was so thick with dust that his desert boots left fluted prints. Two starving dogs, one with a hideous eye infection, scurried out of the lavatories where they had been searching for water. A humid stench hung in the air, a mixture of excrement and decay. The door to the inner offices lay open and Alexander entered. Inside the smell was worse than that from the lavatories. Clouds of flies buzzed in the gloom; they landed on his damp face and arms, as if his fresh sweat was the reason that they had been gathering. Alexander flicked on a light switch but nothing happened. 'Blast,' he muttered and swatted a fat fly with the palm of his hand and brushed its black oozing carcass from his skin.

He opened another door and almost immediately slammed it. 'Ken . . . Mike,' he yelled. The cameraman and the sound man turned from where they had been leaning against the Land Rover in the shade and ran towards Alexander's voice. They found him in a frenzy, attempting to rid himself of the flies that crawled over him, trying to enter the corners of his mouth and nose and ears and eyes. They swarmed down the collar of his bush shirt and he squashed them against his torso.

The two men reopened the inner door. The sight and smell of the swollen corpses of two khaki-uniformed game wardens caused Ken to retch. He staggered outside and threw up. Immediately the dogs roused themselves and ambled over to lick his vomit from the dust. The driver got out and, seeing the state of the man, fetched a water bottle. Alexander and Mike returned to the Land Rover, pursued by flies. 'Get in,' they whispered to Ken and the driver, fearing that they were being watched. The noise from the engine of the vehicle seemed to have increased its volume and the men felt exposed and vulnerable as they drove on into the jungle scrub.

Half a mile further down a track a wooden bungalow stood in a clearing, raised above the ground on piles. Outside was a peeling painted notice, on which could just be read, CHIEF WARDEN'S RESIDENCE. There was no sign of life. A mongoose thundered across the roof and scurried away into the bush and a huge monitor lizard edged its way ponderously between the supports beneath the building. The birds in the trees made sounds like tin cans being rattled and a hornbill squawked on the wing out of sight. There was an eerie silence from the bungalow.

Nervously the three men walked across some logs that bridged an animal pit surrounding the house to take a closer look. Alexander took out the piece of paper on which he had written the name of the Chief Warden, and called out several times. There was no sign of life. Unwilling to climb the steps and make a closer investigation for fear of ambush, he stood at a distance and called out again. Nothing. Despondent, they were about to leave when there were sounds of a vehicle approaching from another direction along a dirt track. Nervous, unable to judge just what was happening at the reserve and by now quite fearful and anticipating the possibility of trouble, they returned to their own vehicle and driver. Towards them in a cloud of red dust came an open-topped Jeep. Inside were two men wearing wardens' uniforms, both carrying automatic weapons, bandoliers hanging across their shoulders. Alexander was unnerved; he would have expected them to have high-velocity rifles with sights if they had been genuine trackers. They got down from their ramshackle Jeep smiling, weapons in hands. Alexander likewise got down and he too smiled as he took a step towards them.

'Sir Alexander Haye, here to film with official government permission.'

'Papers?' demanded one of the men, still grinning. His teeth were stained red from chewing betel nuts. Alexander unbuttoned the breast pocket of his sleeveless jacket and unfolded his documents for them. A fly crawled out from its hiding place and took flight. It landed on the trigger finger of the other man, where it started to preen its wings. His finger flicked it away. The party watched nervously as the first man peered at the paperwork with the halting intensity of someone who was unable to read. Alexander, Ken and Mike flashed the plastic identity cards with coloured photographs of themselves that were pinned to their shirts. These too were scrutinised.

'We're here to film elephants,' said Alexander, hoping that the way to deal with these two was with the arrogance and confidence of officialdom. He was about to mention the names of the President and the Minister of the Environment, but hesitated. Depending on which party they owed allegiance to, voicing the wrong name might be sufficient for these trigger-happy thugs to shoot them all where they stood. He left the papers to do their work. The men seemed to be satisfied and the documents were returned to Alexander.

'You follow. We take you to elephant.' Grinning shiftily at one another the two bandits slapped their right hands one on the other in a triumphal gesture, whooping and yowling hysterically as they returned to their Jeep. In the back lay a booty of freshly killed animals, heaped upon great curved tusks of ivory, scarcely concealed by a tarpaulin.

Alexander, Ken and Mike got back into their Land Rover and the driver started up its engine. They sorted their video and sound equipment and prepared themselves for filming. No one trusted these men after the killings at the reserve offices, but they followed. They were there to film what was probably the last herd of mature breeding elephants in the world. The idea of this television scoop was sufficient to suppress some of their fear and turn it into excitement. They followed the red dust cloud deeper and deeper into jungle.

The sun was getting low and after an hour of trailing in huge circles along cratered tracks, thorn bushes scratching their arms, with nothing more than the odd jungle fowl to be seen, they were becoming increasingly convinced that they were being led into a situation of extreme danger. It had become apparent from their erratic driving that the men were high on some narcotic and possibly seeking further kicks from this pantomime. Alexander was about to direct their driver to turn back when the leading vehicle abruptly turned and led them out into a vast clearing some acres across. They bumped over the cracked surface of a dried-up waterhole for another mile. Alexander and the crew became increasingly nervous. There was absolute silence. Just a desert of caked mud, reddening with the rays of the setting sun. Ken muttered that it was too late to film. Alexander tried to encourage them. At least if they discovered the location of the herd they could return at dawn and get in a full day. All of them feared an ambush.

A shout. The trackers stopped their Jeep and signalled for them to get down. Alexander held back.

'Where are the elephants?'

The two men indicated with their guns. In the fast

receding twilight Alexander and his crew stared at what looked like an outcrop of smooth rocks, bluish-white streaks on their surface glowing in the last light. Cautiously they approached.

'See, elephant, there elephant . . . there.' They pointed their guns at the outcrop. The leader of the two men raised his voice.

'You,' he addressed Alexander, 'I find you elephant.' He extended his hand with palm open. His grinning jaws parted and he began to laugh maniacally.

'Dollars,' he demanded.

Alexander took out some banknotes and gave them to the man. He turned from Alexander to Ken and Mike, raising his machine-gun under his arm from where it hung on its strap over his shoulder.

'Dollars!' he said again and clicked off the safety catch. Each of them hurriedly fumbled in their pockets for more banknotes. His hand closed on them as if a trap had been sprung. The two men then backed away, the barrels of their guns trained on the frightened group of Englishmen, leapt back into their Jeep and sped away.

Slowly the rocks seemed to re-arrange themselves. The sun set as a circle of fire under a band of cloud that looked like a grey pall of smoke on the horizon. Then came a sweet acrid smell on the evening air. For as far as they could see on the banks of the waterhole lay elephants. Dead and mutilated elephants. Their tusks had been sawn from their heads, leaving bloody rivers down their scarred trunks. Tiny eyes, some open and staring out under straggly lashes, some lidded and sunk into their sockets. Beneath their bellies their ribs thrust unnaturally up into the air, forming huge curved mounds of flesh, straining under their wrinkled, mud-crusted skin. Their legs and shoulders jutted out at obtuse angles, soft feet showing their padded undersides to the night air. Birdshit glowed in chalky white streaks across their immense carcasses. On the fringe of the massacre something moved.

Alexander felt a wave of panic rise up from his stomach, flutter uneasily in his breast and tingle in his scalp; the other two men froze. One of the elephants was not yet dead but lay wounded; beside it stood a baby caressing it with its trunk. They moved closer. The huge elephant started and fanned its ragged veined ears against the glow on the horizon. The baby pushed its trunk between its mother's forelegs, raised its mouth and began to suckle at her breast. The mother's thin tail swished up in the air and she let out a terrible cry and struggled to her feet before sinking down and collapsing over on to her side; her trunk arched and curled towards her infant, which nuzzled against her flank.

Alexander thought of his elephant alone at the zoo and tears rolled down his cheeks, silently, for the folly he had committed. He thought of the baby, his besotted keeper beside him, being taken from his caged and moated paddock to walk amongst the crowds who had come for the show. The chattering faces of men, women and children watching with delight as the young beast was paraded and performed for them. Unknowing that they were blessed to see the last elephant ever to reside at London Zoo. He turned away from the misery and left the graveyard to its predators.

Outside on the rest-house veranda Olivia and Bess, girlfriend of Mike, the film crew's sound man, were sitting together in candlelight waiting for Alexander and Ken and Mike to return. In the darkness under a tangled clump of bougainvillaea a family of scrawny, tiger-striped tabby cats tumbled about hunting cicadas and other insects, which on capture they devoured with small crunching noises. The mother cat emerged nervously from time to time, having caught sight of the large platter of sandwiches on the table in front of the two women. Olivia hissed at the cat and she retreated and hid surreptitiously, keeping her huge amber eyes fixed on the food. The rustlings from the cats added to the restlessness that Bess felt as her fears mounted for the men. It was two hours after sunset and there was still no sign of them. She found that her imagination was elaborating ever more fantastic and dangerous scenarios which, as each appeared in the forefront of her mind, she attempted to suppress and tried to convince herself that all would be well.

Olivia, as ever, appeared in complete control. Faced with such calm, Bess felt unable to give voice to her anxiety and sat tensely on the edge of her uncomfortable wicker chair, pressing her hands between her knees. Her naturally curly hair had tightened into an unruly tangle in the humid air and trails of sweat streaked the powder she had put on her face to stop it shining. Bess felt wet between her thighs and her denim jeans had become tight and uncomfortable.

Olivia looked immaculate in a pressed linen safari suit. She was wearing a creamy ivory necklace round her throat and silver-decorated ivory bangles on her wrists, which clicked lightly together as she reached out for her glass of warm beer and sipped. In the monochrome golden glow of the candlelight she looked to Bess like a 1930s fashion plate. Bess lifted the linen cloth that was draped over the sandwiches and tossed one in the direction of the bougainvillaea. It fell short. The mother cat pounced on it and started to drag it back towards the bush. Her starving kittens scrambled towards the feast, hissing and spitting, fighting with one another for their share.

Olivia turned to Bess and arched one eyebrow and in a low, controlled voice said, 'That was a mistake.'

Bess sensed a cold chill pass over the surface of her damp flesh. Minutes later she felt utterly humiliated as she realised that they were surrounded on the raised veranda by a score of starving cats.

No one stirred when the men returned to the rest house. The lights were out and all that could be seen was the occasional flicker of candlelight from various points deep within the open building. There was nobody in reception and seemingly nothing moved. Their driver left them hurriedly and went to his quarters.

Alexander called out. The man who had welcomed them when they first arrived emerged carrying a torch. Its weak light went out and the man slammed it down on the reception counter. It relit. He said nothing but took out their keys, tossed them into the dim oval beam, then scurried away with his fading lamp into a dark room beyond.

Alexander realised that these people had all known what had been happening at the reserve and were too frightened to talk. No doubt someone had issued a warning. He called after the retreating man.

'I want to make a telephone call.'

'Lines down, sir.' The man came forward.

'Since when?'

The man shrugged. 'It happens.'

'Terrorists?' queried Alexander.

'It happens,' repeated the man.

Alexander was about to get angry. He wanted to call the capital; to report the situation at the reserve. The murder of the two officials and massacre of the elephants. But he checked himself. There was something in the sheepish fear of the man, in the isolation of the guest house, that stopped him.

Olivia turned her head, she had heard Alexander's voice coming from reception. Bess, overwhelmed at seeing Mike, got up and rushed forward to give him a kiss.

He put his arm round her waist and held her close to his side.

'There's no one in the kitchen,' she said. 'Everyone seems to have deserted us, besides that guy in reception. He gave me keys to the bar. Made us some sandwiches ... This power cut ... Mike, Mike, these people, they seem afraid of something.'

Bess, in her absolute relief that they were all returned safely, felt her face colour as a rush of heat swamped her. They followed her out on to the veranda, where she seated herself in the chair furthest away from Olivia.

Olivia looked up at Alexander. 'Hello, darling. You're late.'

'Here, I'll fetch you all some cooler beer,' said Bess. She leapt up again and went over to the bar to collect some more mugs and bottles for the men.

'Have you finished filming?' asked Olivia tartly. 'I can't be expected to spend another night in this bloody hole.'

'Thank you, Bess,' Alexander said, and took a gulp of his beer.

'Well?' Olivia tightened her lips. The necklace and bangles glowed against her white skin.

Alexander stared at her. Her petulance and hostility under the circumstances enraged him. When he noticed the ivory jewellery that she was wearing he leant forward and in a low voice breathed, 'Take them off ... the baubles.' Olivia, confused, clasped her hand to her throat. 'I don't want you wearing them.'

The others listened nervously to the anger in Alexander's voice.

'These?' exclaimed Olivia. 'What is it, Alexander? You, you bought them for me!' The level of her voice rose to a strangled squeak.

'I know,' he said, letting out a long sigh, 'and now I want you to take them off.'

Olivia looked at him sullenly. 'Suddenly got a conscience?' she sneered. But looking directly into his face she began to unclasp the trinkets and sulkily threw them down on the table. They landed in a pool of foamy spilt beer. Bess clutched Mike's hand and he squeezed it tight.

'How was the filming? Did you find the elephants?'

'Bess, I ... I'm sorry, we're all a little shaken,' said Alexander apologetically.

'What is it? Tell me.' The girl leant forward sympathetically.

Alexander was still looking hard at Olivia. Then he cast his eyes from side to side as if someone might be listening behind them. 'They were dead,' he said in a whisper.

'No!' exclaimed Bess.

'All of them, dead,' sighed Alexander sadly.

'Drought?'

'Slaughtered ... bulls, cows, infants, slaughtered ... ivory for arms.'

'We found two dead wardens,' interjected Mike. 'I've never ...'

'Shut up!' said Alexander, lowering his voice even

103

further. 'They all know why we are here. They know what we've seen. We're a threat. Some more beer, Bess. Since you've taken over the bar.'

'You see, I'm right. We must get out, tonight,' said Olivia, still smarting.

'Not a chance. We'd run straight into an ambush,' snapped Alexander. 'Uncover those sandwiches and laugh . . . someone, laugh.'

The cats, who had gained courage while everyone's attention had been diverted, had moved closer in the gloom. Suddenly two of them, who had been poised in a crouch on top of the veranda rail, leapt through the air and landed on top of the sandwiches on the table. Bess screamed as the creatures flew past her, knocked the glass out of Mike's hand and smashed it on to the floor. The cache of ivory slid about in the pool of beer and the cats ran off with their prizes clasped between their teeth.

Olivia regained her composure, smirked and muttered under her breath, 'Little fool.'

Inside the rest house the man in reception was roused from where he slumbered in a corner of his room by a mosquito. He sank back on to his camp bed.

They wouldn't be any trouble. Anyway, he was no friend of the terrorists, or the army. He shifted his position and slept.

At dawn, despite protests from both Olivia and Bess,

the men drove out once again to the reserve, leaving them behind at the rest house. Much of the fear of the night before seemed to have lifted as the morning sounds of birds and monkeys crescendoed through the treetops. Alexander and the crew were all in an ebullient mood, for each had realised that they could turn the film round. This would not just be another film of the ivory trade and its brutal effects on the numbers and structure of elephant herds. What they had witnessed the previous day was the massacre of the last known herd of elephants in Asia, perhaps in the world. From this brutish calamity they could produce a film that would win each of them fame. This was to be a prizewinner. Alexander thought of his 'baby' waiting for him at London Zoo.

When they approached the gates of the reserve much of their animation departed. Standing astride the entrance, with guns pointing straight at them, were three uniformed men.

'Roll camera. Keep it turning over,' instructed Alexander.

Trembling with excitement, Ken did as he was asked. Their driver slowed down and stopped the Land Rover some hundred yards from the men, who appeared to be police. He turned round to Ken and signalled to him to keep the camera hidden. Alexander got down with his hands raised and stood quite still beside the vehicle. The three armed men did not move. The small sinister click of them simultaneously cocking their automatic weapons could be heard clearly. Hands still raised above his head, tentatively Alexander started to walk towards the policemen. They lowered the muzzles of their weapons and the man standing in the centre broke rank and started to approach Alexander. He smiled. A sigh of relief came from those in the vehicle as they watched Alexander shaking the hand of the policeman. The other two returned to guard the offices.

Alexander went back to the Land Rover for their documents. He whispered under his breath, 'Act as if this is the first time we've come here. Say nothing of yesterday, the wardens, the men. Nothing. We want no part in this.'

The police let them go on their way. They were preoccupied by the murder of the wardens. Alexander proposed that they get the filming done as quickly as possible before any interrogations took place. They should collect Olivia and Bess and get out of the area altogether.

When they located the dead elephants daylight stripped some immediate misery from the scene. The baking sun had dried their blood and vultures stood ranged along their backs like a gruesome Greek chorus at the scene of a tragedy. The orphaned baby was nowhere to be seen. Ken shot all his film and Alexander recorded the scene in as much detail as he could muster. Last checks were made. 'Wrap,' said Ken. 'We've got a winner.'

Five

It was Sunday morning. A faint mist hung over the island. Sleepy signs of life were coming from the village. The man who ran the stall on the roadside was taking down its wooden shutters, placing jars of brightly coloured sweets on the counter and hanging up bunches of red, green and yellow bananas. Two men passed along the shore on bicycles, the spokes of their wheels glittering in the early morning sun. A woman steadied a basket on her head with one hand and with the other held on to a small child in a flowered frock. Some dogs were scavenging along the shoreline, where the storm had thrown up dead fish and crabs. Between split husks of king coconut shiny crows were flocking, jabbing their tough black beaks into the milky white flesh. An occasional scuffle broke out between the dogs and the crows as they competed for the richest pickings on the beach. Around Max's tower a flock of bright green parakeets was chattering in the branches of a temple tree, and the 'tin can bird' rattled out its morning cry. Small monkeys whooped their chorus at the dawn.

Downstairs in the Hall of the Lotus Jaquitta was still in darkness and did not stir; she just ruffled her feathers from time to time in response to the sounds of the birds outside.

On the deserted beach below Thomas and Maria slid the boat down the sand and into the water. They paddled the few yards across the calm strait to the island. Thomas looked out anxiously for any sign of damage after the storm. About the landing stage debris had gathered, plastic bottles bobbed on the surface, caught in a tangle of vegetation and driftwood, surrounded by dirty yellow foam. The path and steps to the house were littered with shredded leaves that had been ripped from the trees and the occasional broken branch. The shutters of the house were still tightly bolted and only the door to the garden cavern lay open, half torn off its hinges, a puddle of water outside its entrance. They went into the kitchen and Thomas started to lay the fire. Maria tied her starched white apron around her waist and secured her cap to her hair with red plastic pins. She knelt down and began her prayers. Solemnly and silently Thomas went out to fetch more wood and a fresh can of kerosene. He stopped inside the garden cavern for a moment, sat down on a stone ledge and rolled himself a cigarette, lit it and drew breath. He could still hear the sound of Maria saying her rosary in the kitchen. He took these moments for himself as the repetitive rhythm gnawed away at the back of his brain.

When they had arrived at the orphanage the main gates had been locked and soldiers stood outside armed with machine-guns. Through the chain-link fence they could just see into the compound, which was puddled and muddy from the heavy rain. It was full of military vehicles, some with Red Cross flags slapping against canvas awnings in the wind. Frightened and confused by this unexpected sight, Thomas went up to one of the guards and asked for Father Miguel. The man said nothing, but pointed his gun in the direction of a side entrance next to a low open building that was used as a classroom. Nervously, Thomas took Maria's hand and they made their way along the track. Just as they reached the gate a vehicle sped out, splashing them both with muddy water.

They walked towards the open-sided school building. From the classroom they heard a quiet commotion. In the subdued light the room was seething with people, hunched over small bodies which were lying on the long wooden tables that had served as desks. No one noticed them, too absorbed with attending to wounded children. In the gloom they caught sight of a priest. It was not Father Miguel. The young man was leaning over the body of a small boy aged about six dressed in the uniform that school-age children wore: little navy blue cotton shorts and a white shirt. The child's shiny dark hair lay in a fringe across his forehead above his closed eyes. Long black eyelashes rested on his cheeks.

The priest anointed the child, then took hold of both his tiny hands and pressed his palms and fingers together as if at prayer on top of his chest, revealing a terrible open wound under his armpit which gaped through his ripped cotton shirt. Maria closed her eyes and turned away. These children had been butchered. Half of them were already dead and others were squirming and crying pitifully at their injuries. Another Red Cross vehicle pulled up. A nun and a woman doctor lifted two small girls, their bodies as light as wisps of hay, on to the same stretcher and loaded them into a Jeep. The nun jumped in beside the wounded children, stroking their hair and soothing them with the soft sound of her voice. Numbly Thomas led Maria towards Father Miguel's office. They were stopped at the door by the presence of two nuns who were kneeling on the pyal outside, deep in prayer. One raised her eyes to Thomas and recognised him. She stood up.

'Father Miguel, dead. They came during Benediction. They shot him where he stood. Father José Maria and sister Sophia . . . the children . . . all dead. Holy martyrs.'

She fell down upon her knees as if no longer able to support her own weight and buried her face in her dusty black skirts. The gold band on her finger glinted as her fingers hurried over the surface of the jet beads of her rosary.

Speechless with horror they turned away. From the

other side of the compound the young priest came out, carrying the boy across his outspread forearms, and placed his wretched little corpse down upon a wet canvas sheet on the ground, side by side with several other bodies. Small barefoot brown legs lay close together where they jutted out from beneath the hems of their uniforms. Thomas looked down at the line of dead children and the last confused remnants of his belief in God utterly deserted him.

Thomas stubbed his cigarette out under his foot and leant down to pick up a yellow piece of paper that lay on the floor. It was covered in Chinese characters. He smoothed it out, folded it carefully away into his pocket and returned to the kitchen. Silently, together, Thomas and Maria started preparing lunch.

Pyhia arrived early to make up rooms for the guests. She went into the bathrooms and removed woodlice, scorpions and snakes that had crawled up drains and overflows during the storm. In one she found a small harmless viper curled up in a corner. On Maria's instruction she did not enter Max's quarters.

Two Land Rovers pulled up beside the beach opposite Max's island and hooted their horns. Thomas rowed over to collect the luggage which was being set down, and with the help of some village children carried it down to the beach and loaded it into the boat. They stood grinning, waiting for trinkets for their service. Bess took some biros, sweets and coins from her bag and shared them amongst the outstretched hands.

'It's extraordinary,' trilled Bess in excitement, looking across the strait. 'An enchanted island.'

'Yes . . . quite extraordinary,' said Olivia slowly, as if trying to take in the implications of her imminent meeting with Max.

'Oh, it's heavenly,' said Bess, who started to strip down to her shorts and T-shirt. She looked at Thomas. 'Is it safe to wade across?'

'Oh, indeed, Miss, always safe.'

'Come on, Mike . . . let's go.'

The two young people ran down the sand and into the ocean. Ken followed. Alexander and Olivia climbed into the flat-bottomed boat.

Alexander was in a turbulent mood. The horror of the scenes he had witnessed at the game reserve during filming and the tension between him and Olivia had left him in a morose and thoughtful state. But, as Thomas paddled the boat through the clear shallows towards the sanctuary of Max's island, he began to feel tranquil at the prospect of several somnulent days in this paradise. He looked at Olivia; she was not wearing the necklace, but she was cold and somewhat haughty with Thomas about the awkwardness of travelling in the boat piled with luggage. Olivia's arrogant superiority towards servants had always embarrassed Alexander. He tried to compensate with friendly chatter, but Thomas remained distracted and exaggeratedly solicitous.

Their suitcases were unloaded on to the landing stage. It took two more journeys to ferry all the equipment across to the island. Exhausted, Thomas climbed the steps laden with luggage and met them in the Hall of the Lotus.

'Where's Max?' enquired Olivia as he entered.

'He will be in the tower, your ladyship,' said Thomas. 'I have not seen him as yet this morning. Here, see, he has left a note for you, Sir Alexander.'

Sitting on the table was a white sealed envelope addressed to Alexander. Olivia paced around the circular room. Jaquitta watched her, revolving her head until it faced backwards, then she turned on her perch and eyed the woman on the rest of her transit around the room back to where Alexander was standing.

'I'm going to have a shower. I can't tell you what hell the last few days have been, Thomas. Such a relief to be here. Come, Olivia.' Alexander picked up the envelope, looked at it and put it back on the table. 'Thank you, Thomas, we won't disturb Max. See you at lunch. Show us to our room?'

From below came the sound of the others' laughter as they came up the steps outside.

Inside their room Alexander pulled off all his clothes and lay down on the bed. He watched as the mahogany fan above his head whirled, clicking every so often on its uneven path. His return to Max's territory plunged him back into the turmoil of their nursery battles. On their

113

seventh birthday, as so often happened, they were given a single present between the two of them. Because the boys were twins, aunts and godparents alike had the mistaken idea that they should share everything. The present was a Noah's Ark. Alexander had wanted one so much. The Ark was unwrapped and despite the label clearly worded 'To Maximilian and Alexander from Great-aunt Letty', he presumed that it was his. A terrible fight broke out and in order to resolve it their mother said that the Ark should be Max's and the wooden animals Alexander's. The boys were satisfied. But Alexander remembered how he had never been allowed by Max to put his animals into the Ark. And how content his brother had been with the empty Ark.

He listened as Olivia took her shower; to the water slapping down on to the mosaic tiled floor and trickling away down the drain. When the noise stopped Olivia opened the door and a gush of moist air flowed out and steamed up the looking glass on the other side of the room.

'Olivia,' he said, 'when we get back, I'm thinking of . . .' He heard the sound of her brushing her hair. 'Yes . . .' He paused, the idea had only just come to him and he was reasoning aloud. 'I could go back to research. A post at . . . perhaps, Oxford. We could buy a house, it's not far from London, you could still see your friends, have them to stay. I feel so confined in that flat. An old rectory, Oxfordshire, you know the kind of thing. Large garden . . .' He went on painting an

114

increasingly intricate picture of their future as he dozed on top of the bed.

There was silence from Olivia. She listened to every word he said as she brushed her long black curls, tweaking at them until they lost their limpness and sprang back to life about her face. She carefully re-applied her make-up, came back into the room and dressed in a startlingly white cotton frock. Alexander had drifted into sleep. She glanced across the room at a portrait of Max on the wall. Exasperated by her husband she shook Alexander out of his torpor. He opened his eyes and the smile that was on his lips left as he saw her hard and angry face leaning over him. Her dark red mouth snarled at him. She threw back her head and started screeching at the top of her voice.

'If you think that I am going to live the rest of my life with you in some provincial backwater, making hedgerow bloody jam and filling lavender bags . . . entertaining dons' wives and earnest researchers to sherry just because you've had your conscience rattled by a few dead elephants.' She paused and started to pace the room. Then she turned and looked again, up at the portrait.

'It's Max, isn't it? Isn't it? As soon as you two come within reach of one another you get more and more like him. What the hell did you think was happening here? You should have known that this wasn't a picnic. There's virtually a bloody war going on. Oh yes . . . just because Sir Alexander Haye has to confront something he doesn't quite like, which doesn't fit the script, what does he think of? Resigning. Well, resign. Resign from the whole bloody lot.'

Alexander got up. He could bear no more. He went to the bathroom and slammed the door. Turned on the water and tried to drown the sound of Olivia's voice. She banged on the door.

'You, you and Max, you're both incapable of facing reality. Look at this ridiculous house. Just look at it. This island, the whole set-up. If I were those bloody guys out there in the jungle, this would be the first place I'd torch. And Max, and you, and all of us with it. To hell with you, the parsonage, Oxford. What does it matter about the massacre of a few drought-stricken elephants? Men, women and children are dying out there.'

Alexander stayed behind the locked door.

'You sicken me. Both of you.' Olivia turned to the glass, wiped the steam away with a sweep of her hand and threaded a pair of earrings through her lobes.

'I'm going downstairs. I need a drink. I'll dig Max out of his ivory tower. It's about time someone did. And if you or that bloody obsequious servant and his born-again wife . . .'

Alexander listened as Olivia stormed away.

Bess and Mike were so delighted with their shaded room, the flowers, the terrace, the view of the ocean and the palm trees beyond that they fell into one another's arms. They heard the commotion from the next room.

'I can't imagine why Olivia stays with Alexander, she seems to hate him so much,' said Mike.

'She likes being Lady Haye.' Bess pulled her beloved towards her and kissed him.

'Is that enough?'

'No, she's just trapped, I suppose.'

'So are you,' said Mike and pulled her down on to the bed.

In an adjoining room Ken retreated from the noise and, having asked Thomas to bring him a drink, went out on to his terrace. He stretched himself out on a planter's chair under the shade of a hibiscus and watched the beads of condensation slither down his icy glass. He thought of his camera equipment. He would attend to cleaning it later.

At two o'clock a gong sounded from the hall and they all assembled for drinks except Olivia, who had found a bottle of whisky, filled a tumbler and set off to find Max.

Thomas had prepared an exquisite cocktail of lurid tropical fruits. Jaquitta piped and trilled her repertoire at her assembled audience.

Outside the sky clouded over and the waves started to break their white foam upon one another. The humidity and temperature increased. The monsoon rains lurked behind the headland, waiting to make their return.

Olivia went first to Max's bedroom. The blinds were

still drawn and the shutters fastened. There was a smell of sickness in the air. She saw the pile of tangled sheets on the bed and went to touch them. They were still damp and smelt slightly of sweat. She noticed the yellow semen stains. It was like entering a room after a night of lust. She smiled to herself. The girl, Pyhia, she had seen how pretty she was. Olivia liked intruding on his secret, it gave her the edge. She closed the door and went outside to where she had left the bottle of whisky, refilled her glass and sat down.

'So that's what Max has been up to . . . a furtive affair with a native.' She smiled at his weakness. Then felt slightly cheated. Max, she believed, had always continued to want her. At university she had ended their affair and taken up with Alexander, for some time she kept him unaware of her new relationship with his brother. She liked to sleep with him from time to time. It was her trick on the twins. She had ebbed and flowed between them, a hard-shelled creature whom each desired. In their twinship she saw weakness, as if each were half the man. Although she had settled for Alexander, part of her still longed to possess Max. Across his wide ocean he was still a wind blowing back in her face, a mysterious rasping echo that rushed past her ears calling out, not to her, but to his brother. The scent of him was ever-present in her nostrils. So she stood stranded on her rocky pinnacle, but however sweetly she sang her tunes of enticement, she was only able to grasp a fragment of each. Resentment grumbled up through her until it shrieked itself free. Left with bitterness and malice, she held the two brothers in contempt for their fragile bond. Only once since their affair had Max tried to make love to her. Drunk, he had pleaded with her to leave Alexander and come and live with him. In that confused and hapless moment she had believed him, deluded herself that she had power over both the twins. It was comforting to think of Max alone, desiring her.

Pyhia passed by on a terrace below, her faded blue robe blowing about in the breeze. Olivia studied her with renewed curiosity. Yes, she was exquisite, she thought, and took another swig at her drink.

Alexander joined the others in the Hall of the Lotus. He was certain that they must have overheard Olivia, but he behaved as if nothing had happened. Thomas entered the room and announced that lunch was served.

'Where's Olivia?' asked Alexander nervously. 'Max too.'

'Shall go to call them, sir.' Thomas retreated in the direction of the tower.

He took the winding track between the canna lilies. Their brilliant red flowers looked ragged after the storm. There was no point in his clearing the paths, for another downpour was imminent. Ever-increasing volumes of cloud gathered in the sky. When he reached the upper terrace he noticed, scattered about, string and straw and torn yellow paper covered with Chinese characters, just like the shred he had picked up off the floor of the garden cavern. It was littered between the plants and caught up in the thorn palms. As he turned a corner he stopped, for directly in his path stood an extraordinary shrub, unlike anything that he had seen growing on Mannar before. It was about six feet tall with multiple bare stems each crowned with black flowers of intricate petalage already wilting in the tropical heat. Thomas was unnerved by this plant, so out of place in his familiar landscape.

As he reached the steps to the tower he found Olivia sitting drunkenly at the foot, outside the door.

'Come to find the master, have we?' she said in a mocking tone.

'Lunch is served, your ladyship.' Thomas stepped past her, ignoring her sarcasm, intent on finding Max.

'You're . . . wasting . . . your . . . time,' Olivia slurred, singing the word 'time'. 'He's dead. Did you hear me? Dead . . . dead, you foolish man. Dead as a dodo. Stone-dead. Brain-splattered . . . dead.'

Thomas looked down, horrified by the drunken woman.

She laughed. 'You don't get me, do you?' She still sung her words, spun them through her drunkenness as if the mocking sing-song would ameliorate despair. Then started to sob.

'Go on, then, see for yourself, but I tell you he's dead.'

She got up slowly. There was a muddy stain on the back of her pristine white frock. With deliberate movements she smoothed the creases from its skirt. Then she ruffled her hair and brushed the tears from her cheeks.

'I'm sorry, Thomas, I didn't mean . . .' She stood aside.

He entered the tower and climbed the spiral staircase to the top.

Max lay slumped in his chair, limbs in unbalanced chaos, his head lolling to one side, his legs sprawled out under his kaftan. A tattered mess of flesh where his face used to be. There was blood everywhere. Unable to find any other way to deal with his emotions, Thomas crossed himself and started to breathe out in nervous reflex, 'Hail Mary, full of grace, the Lord be with you. Blessed art thou amongst women . . . and blessed is the fruit of thy womb, Jesus.' Chanted over and over, the prayer became jumbled. He noticed the gun where it lay on the floor. Drops of blackened blood spread like ink stains on the blotter on the desk.

'Holy Mary, Mother of God . . .' As he edged forward in the stillness, there was a faint smell as the wind through the open door disturbed the curdled air.

'Pray for us sinners, now and at the hour of our death.'

As the word 'death' was on his lips, he fell to his knees and continued desperately to chant the rosary for the dead man's soul. Overwhelmed as he was, Thomas could not avoid the fact that Max had died by his own hand, not in a state of grace.

Outside Olivia had fled wailing back towards the house. Her cry resounded through the underground caverns. It was caught by seabirds while it hurried

121

along terraces and fluttered in the tops of the palms; it turned the spiral staircase and twisted up the tower, where, trapped in the turret room, it echoed around the slumped body at the desk. It rang against the bell jar, where the anopheles mosquitoes were trapped, the flat pads of their feet scrabbling against its glass.

Alexander arrived. Thomas was still on his knees, trembling, frenziedly repeating his prayers in an attempt to save Max's soul from torment. Alexander looked at Max. He felt utterly forlorn. A captive of the sickening horror that was before him. Then suddenly there was a surge of violent energy from inside his body. His heart pounded and his muscles tensed. He struck out at the bell jar. It shattered. The mosquitoes flew out and danced. Sang out their high-pitched whine as they droned in circles about the corpse. 'Damned fool,' he yelled, then turned away, went over to the half-crazed man and helped him to his feet. Shaking with rage he led him down from the tower to the kitchen.

Maria was near to tears, desperately attending the fire, which was blowing back on the monsoon wind, covering everything with smuts. Alexander left them in the smoky room and went to find Ken and Mike, who were already seated with Bess at the lunch table. All three were merry and giggling together in the shady dining room.

Alexander hesitated at the mouth of the cave. All three looked up nervously and waited for him to speak. Behind him the smoke from the kitchen billowed out through the door and snatches of murmured prayer resounded in his ears. He looked in at the painted walls of the cave with their fugitive colours that had lost their brilliance. At the bleached and powdery skies where the birds that flew in them were no more than etched marks; at the once green hills and jungle trees of faded blue. The ochre-painted animals still glowed, sharp and well defined, but the herd of elephants that stood around the lake was nothing more than a shadowy outline. The gods had lost their charmed pipes and nymphs their robes and garlands. The arcadian fresco of the legendary history of Mannar was reduced to a near monochrome of dusty plaster.

A low explosive noise came from the village, quickly followed by shorter, more violent sounds. Any semblance of elation in their mood left them and they sat around the table with their breath drawn, their eyes bright with fear. They listened.

Shells and mortars exploded, backed by continuous streams of machine-gun fire. A billowing pall of smoke whirled into the sky. Fire started to rage amongst the trees, fanned by a strengthening monsoon wind. People fled out from between palm trees, across the road and down on to the beach, where they launched their fishing boats, catamarans and canoes, fighting with one another for a place in the vessels. The little wooden provision stall was ablaze and black smoke weaving about in the wind. Craft set sail towards Max's island like a fleeing armada. Men, women and children swam after the boats, dipping and rising through the waves like a shoal of porpoise. As they reached the island the boats divided into two fleets and passed by on either side towards the rocks on the southern side. The swimmers were caught in these heavier waters. They were tossed by the waves and dispersed in all directions. Most drowned and their bodies were carried away on currents far out into the ocean.

Downstairs Olivia, coddled by alcohol, oblivious to anything, entered the Hall of the Lotus. Jaquitta eyed her. She went to the side table where Max had left the envelope for Alexander and studied the handwriting; it was identical to Alexander's. Olivia did not open the letter, but slowly tore it into tiny pieces and let it fall as white confetti at her feet. She crossed to the centre of the room and looked closely at the coloured bird through the iron bars of its cage.

Jaquitta lifted her feathers and bowed her head, waiting to be tickled behind her neck, waiting for Max to tickle her behind her neck. Olivia put her huge drunken dark brown eyes to the bars of the bird's cage. Jaquitta shifted nervously along her perch. Olivia moved her eyes to the opposite side of the cage. Jaquitta moved sideways along her perch away from Olivia. Olivia unclasped the barred door. Slowly Jaquitta angled her way down and found her way out. She fluttered her wings and landed on the heavy brass bell-handle on the top of her cage. Olivia clapped her hands. The sound cracked the air, resonated around the room. She clapped her hands again. Terrified, the bird took flight, out through the open door, and was not seen again.

*   *   *

They buried Max's body on the southern side of his island, where it faced the endless ocean. No priest, no official could be found. All coffins had been used for the village dead, so they wrapped his body in a shroud and delivered it straight to the earth.

Olivia dismissed Pyhia. Thomas and Maria returned to the orphanage, which had filled with hundreds of children who had no living relatives and were displaced by terror, hunger and disease. They both dedicated themselves to that work in the name of God.

After the island was deserted and the house closed, decay set in. Homeless villagers who had survived the massacre waded across the strait and looted anything that could be carried away. The ferryboat was taken from its moorings and stood upturned on stilts on the beach, providing shelter for a fisherman and his family who had lost their hut in the holocaust. The papier mâché snail in the tower remained preserved, honeycombed with lacy wormholes. Inner walls were striated by dripping water. Termites infested the rafters, loosening the tiles. They slithered down the roof, leaving gaping holes through which rays of burning sun shone like searchlights on to the floors. The heraldic beasts above the portico fell one by one as the stone balustrade crumbled and lay in broken segments on the ground. Vines and creepers strangled the trees and covered the garden terraces and paths, forming tunnels of bright verdant growth through which green and red parakeets darted and chattered. The tree peony lived on and every spring its flowers opened and spread their black petals. They fell to the ground, splattering like drops of blood. A devilishly fine scent lingered over the island, the scent of the flowers of Hell.

Six

Mosquitoes multiplied and spread like fear, far and wide amongst the already diseased peoples of Mannar. This great breeding swarm sucked at their blood and carried parasites from man to woman to child. No one was spared. Rats and other vermin no longer scurried about unseen but ventured boldly into dwellings, openly scavenged and urinated and defecated. With them they brought a plague that spread so fast among the population that roadsides were illuminated all night with the flames of funeral pyres. The sky glowed orange, and in the daylight the sun was little more than a hazy white glow through the choking smoke rising from the smouldering corpses. In the streets roamed men and women maddened with loss. From the shanty towns and the villages day and night could be heard the wailing sound of mourning. When no help came to the populace to ease its plight, bands of men gathered together and shook their fists in impotent fury at the fates.

From north and south and east and west men and women, half-starved and riddled with disease, set out towards the capital in search of help. Farmers left their animals behind in barren fields, set them free to forage for what they could find. Those already struck down by plague or fever or malnutrition were abandoned, to be ministered to by the old and infirm. Mothers, their milk dried up, carried infants on their backs and walked barefoot beside bullock carts filled with the jumble they had salvaged from their previous lives.

Orphaned children formed lawless gangs and set upon the people at night, robbing them of food and water and blankets. As they walked, they were joined by terrorists who emerged from their secret strongholds. Armed with knives and guns and home-made bombs, with pistols and axes and forks and spades, staves and torches and bare hands, the people marched towards the city.

It was into this anarchy that Alexander, Olivia, Ken, Mike and Bess were plunged as they drove away from Max's island towards the airport. Their driver had absconded with one of their Land Rovers, so they had been forced to pile themselves and as much as was essential into one vehicle.

The atmosphere inside the Land Rover was one of mute calm. No one voiced their fear. Alexander drove, with Ken beside him in the front. Mike sat opposite Olivia, Bess in the back. Bess would have preferred to sit beside Mike, but felt that if she was too close to him she would find it impossible not to show her fright. She longed to cross the space between them and feel his arm around her shoulders. To rest her head on his chest and put her hand in his. But she felt it would have been wrong for her to receive such comfort in their circumstances. She sat, bouncing on the bench, spine rigid, jarring, only her eyes casting about for a possible warning, a glimpse, a sign of anything that might mean danger. Then she drew breath and closed her eyes as she realised that she had no notion, no insight, into what was happening around them. Her anxiety was as useless to her, and to the others, as her ability to apply nail polish.

Alexander had removed the gun that Max had used to shoot himself. It had seemed an object of such import at the time, that lump of machined metal. He could not leave it behind, but once wariness of the power of the object subsided, he picked it up from the blotter with his pocket handkerchief, like a detective in a film, unwilling to leave prints on the gun for fear that he might in some way be implicated in his brother's suicide. He clicked on the safety catch, but did not unload the gun. Later he sat in his room, gazing at it from a distance as it poked out of its linen wrap. He was confounded by the presence of this small instrument of death. Now it lay, still wrapped, in front of him in the glove compartment of the vehicle. The notion came that he might have to take it out, unwrap it, pick it up, superimpose his hand and fingerprints over those of his dead brother and use it once again to kill.

Ken sat sullen and gloomy. He had had to leave much of his treasured camera equipment behind, for there was not room for the five of them and the basic supplies that they needed to get back to the airport. The footage he had shot was stored in an aluminium case under his feet.

The coastal road was empty of motorised traffic. The haze from funeral pyres hung in the shade between the palms, trapped beneath their umbrellas of leaves. Ragged groups of people were camped along the dusty margins of the tarmac. At the sound of the approaching Land Rover they ran out into the road calling for help.

As the islanders marched on towards the capital, they severed power cables and telephone wires, dug trenches across roads, blew up bridges and blocked railway lines. The rich retreated inside their enclaves with their hoards of gold and food and water. They cast their servants on to the streets for fear of dissent from within and tenuously fortified themselves against the howling mob. The people rose against their masters. They stormed their refuges and butchered them all, men, women, children . . . none were spared. Their resentment was so great and their expectations of life so limited that even when they passed through the pathetic shanty towns on the fringes of the city, they looted and pillaged and raped their own. As they streamed onward past the small brick bungalows of the clerical workers, mobs entered those houses and slew entire families.

Finally they torched everything in their wake. All the major arteries into the heart of the capital ran with blood and were ablaze with rivers of fire. The city burned, its heart destroyed by a whirlwind of destruction. Still the populace bayed for more blood. The terrorists, unable to contain the wrath of the people, turned on them, firing their guns into crowds that had gathered together in smouldering squares to listen to their sometime leaders' oratory. The nights resounded with the tic-tac of machine-gun fire and the wails of pye-dogs scampering through the streets, lurking in shadows, scavenging corpses, profiting from demise.

When, finally, the first journalists arrived, they were greeted by lines of ragged refugees. Starving infants and fevered babies cried out weakly. A few of the rich and powerful who had escaped were waiting trembling at the airport and along the quaysides.

The sea was full of ships, fishing boats, launches, sailing dinghies, catamarans and dugout canoes. It looked as if some crazy regatta was in progress within the harbour walls. From quays people scrambled down into any vessel that was moored alongside. In desperation some jumped into the sick, oily water and tried to cling on as the boats left the shore. Overburdened with humanity and luggage, the craft set off, the would-be passengers fighting amongst themselves, pushing one another overboard. In the water struggling bodies held on to bits of driftwood or marker buoys, crying out to gods or man to have mercy upon them and pick them up. Many floundered in the wake of departing boats or were cut to pieces by their propellers. Laden with such numbers survival was impossible as they sailed ever further towards the horizon in their hopeless endeavour to escape. Faced by sickness and overcrowding, on they went blindly towards pirates and typhoons and heat and deprivation. As one man fell foul of another or succumbed to disease he was thrown overboard or, when thirst and starvation finally overtook them, cannibalised.

The journalists scoured the waiting crowd at the airport for a voice. No one would speak, either out of fear or horror at what they had witnessed. There was no political voice to be found rising from the populace, no voice at all, it had been strangled in their throats. Most were empty-eyed and dumb, shuffling in silence. The expressions on the faces of the survivors were frozen in shock. They were the countenances of men, women and children who had had a glimpse into Hell.

But in the capital as soon as the newsmen arrived they found a ready voice. On the steps of the House of Representatives and on street corners rallies were called by self-appointed leaders, who stood on makeshift podiums spitting out rhetoric. There was no one left to attend. Charred and rotting piles of corpses were stacked against buildings by bulldozers. Those would-be politicians stood demented and alone and cried havoc. Their dictatorial voices were amplified by loudspeakers hurriedly strung up between buildings. Martial music played and heroic poetry was recited. Those tunes and rhymes of hope and glory beat upon the eardrums of the dead, who lay in twisted rotting heaps unable to listen to words that would have once sent them delirious with dreams.

When Alexander and Olivia, Ken, Mike and Bess reached the airport it was in turmoil. Some foreign reporters who had arrived on the two charity relief aircraft were walking up and down the line of passengers, waiting without tickets, trying to interview them. The people remained mute and bedraggled. Olivia clutched at Alexander while they all waited to join the next transport out.

Together they walked across the tarmac to the aeroplane. They did not notice the mother elephant, who stood beside the runway bound in chains. A swirling gust of wind eddied. Coloured streamers and marigold petals, which had twined around her legs and feet, rose into the air and were swept away. One of the journalists recognised Alexander and pushed through the crowd.

'Sir, Sir Alexander, Sir Alexander, a photograph with the elephant before you go . . . ?'

Alexander turned and looked at the beast for whose confinement he had in part been responsible. She had pale pink scars on her legs where the constant friction of her chains had worn away her flesh. The offerings had not been swept up and taken away by the holy men, for they had fled. Piles of decomposing herbage lay scattered at her feet. Alexander shook his head at the reporter, turned his back and climbed the aluminium steps to the aeroplane. He shivered feverishly under the monsoon clouds. There was a blast of machine-gun fire. In terror the mother elephant trumpeted. No one heard her above the turmoil.

Alexander gazed out blankly through the smeared perspex window of the aeroplane as it took off into a fiery sunset, then circled above the island before starting its ascent. He stared down at the strait that separated Mannar from its continent. At the dark feathered tops of the palms along its shores. At the orange lights of fires blazing along its highways. As the aircraft banked he thought he glimpsed an iridescent stellar flash in the ocean. He felt a twitch as the thread that joined him to Max broke. He sat huddled in his seat, eyes swollen with tears, vulnerable as an abandoned infant, mewling for an embrace.

Susan Hillmore

THE GREENHOUSE

'Beautifully written, full of charm and a gem of a book'
Daily Telegraph

Vanessa lived still in the remote country home of her childhood. Her parents were dead and her brother had gone; she alone would never leave. Her whole life was invested in the house, the garden and the Greenhouse.

The Greenhouse was a miracle of glass and ironwork, soaring towards the sky. Orchids and tuberoses, nectarines and oranges had flourished inside it while Vanessa's father had been alive. Its golden age was now long past, but Vanessa still lavished care on it and filled it with lilies in bloom. She was planting young vines, preparing them to grow strong under the Greenhouse's protection the day that her life was invaded and damaged forever.

'Strikingly original and powerful...insidiously readable, with a chilling mysticism and brutal magic in its foetid depiction of loss and death. It's an astonishing debut'
Sunday Express

'Hillmore's writing is dense and dappled with colour and light...a novel of strange power'
Independent

VINTAGE